Penguin Books
A Song and Danc

P. J. Kavanagh was born in 1931 in England, and after leaving school worked for a time in Paris. He did his National Service in Korea, where he was wounded. After three years at Merton College, Oxford he taught in Spain and in Java.

His first collection of poems *One and One* came out in 1960, and in 1966 he published an early autobiography *The Perfect Stranger*, which won the Richard Hillary Prize. He has since published two more books of poetry, *On the Way To the Depot* (1967) and *About Time* (1970). His first novel, *A Song and Dance*, won the Guardian Fiction Prize for 1968. He has two small sons and lives mainly in the country. He works as an actor, appearing chiefly on television. He broadcasts regularly by radio and since 1967 has reviewed poetry for the *Guardian*.

P. J. Kavanagh

A Song and Dance

Penguin Books

Penguin Books Ltd, Harmondsworth,
Middlesex, England
Penguin Books Australia Ltd, Ringwood,
Victoria, Australia

First published by Chatto & Windus 1968
Published in Penguin Books 1971

Made and printed in Great Britain by
C. Nicholls & Company Ltd
Set in Linotype Juliana

With love and gratitude to Kate

I

Late on a spring evening in a fashionable quarter of London a young man is sitting with a young woman in front of an electric fire set in a fireplace of surprisingly Moorish appearance.

The room is large, as befits the size of that fireplace, and filled with objects that belong to a period two or three generations before. But they seem to belong there as well, they have been carefully chosen, and with a kind of wit.

About the young man's appearance there is also something archaic although his clothes are normal for the time. His dark-blue corduroy suit is tight-fitting and high-lapelled which gives his jacket the appearance of being a frock-coat. His shirt, startlingly white against the shining depth of his jacket, has a long soft collar that spreads generously, cravat-like, on either side of a broad flowered tie. Between his trousers and his black slip-on shoes cascade, American-fashion, socks that are also very white indeed.

He sits with his feet up on a studded leather sofa which might have escaped from a London club but for the arms at each end which are two foot long mahogany male nudes, full-face and obverse, carved with such care for detail that taken with the size of the sofa they hint at some long-forgotten ducal indelicacies.

Propped on a reading-stand at his side, a brass rod from which swivels a wooden lectern carved in a Pre-Raphaelite fashion, are some typewritten pages which he is reading and correcting with one hand, laughing as he does so.

He has clearly created these surroundings for himself and his dark, almost Italianate appearance, like an Early Victorian Knut: black curls without a parting falling over his white collar and his ears, long lashes, large brown eyes, and along his jawline soft suggestions of fleshiness that give his face a comfortable look.

While he writes and laughs the young woman sews.

There is the sound of the telephone and he jumps to answer it in the hall, obviously delighted by the interruption: a man who enjoys things happening.

His excited voice outside the room contrasts with the stillness of the woman sewing. For a while she goes on and then she stops and stares in front of her – not unhappily, with no particular expression at all. She stays like that even after her husband comes back and is telling her about the call. She nods and smiles, lying back in her chair, but she's clearly 'miles away' as they say, and they who say it would be almost right because the girl, who is me, feels that she is outside the window, looking in, seeing herself and her husband, and that was the tableau she saw.

There are so many things floating about inside us, so many 'selves' – it isn't possible to distinguish all the time which is the most important. You just have to go on until one of them breaks surface and says: 'What about me!' We can move about as much as we like, but if it isn't the right sort of movement other parts of us are biding their time, moving elsewhere, until one day you see things from their angle and nothing looks the same. This is what happened to me at that moment.

I saw I'd been walking for ages on ground I believed would stay solid as long as I didn't look down. Now I did and I was at the edge of a dark hole. This wasn't anybody's fault, maybe not even my own, but there it was. Not the kind of hole you fall through into a whirling Hieronymus Bosch scene; on the contrary, the world was noisy all round but inside the hole itself it was sound-proofed, cork-lined. I only had to slide into it never to hear anything again.

When Simon went to answer the phone I suddenly thought: – If a beautiful naked Christ were to come among us, our circle, all of us, to tell of his vision of the Just City, we'd be polite and respectful of course, but what words could he use to reach us? Anyway there was something dark sucking away under that easy politeness. After a while he'd leave us, go and find people more fertile, more exposed, he'd forget us almost as quickly as we forgot him.

I didn't want to be forgotten like that.

My father was killed in the war. He was rich and I inherited most of his money when I was two. My mother married again, then again, and even he is now an ex-. He is the one I had most to do with, I still see him occasionally at parties given by people twenty years younger than he is. I went to various schools and at these I met people of my own kind – that is to say equivalently well-off – and was happy in a dreamy way. I lived with my mother and her current beau when she was in England, the rest of the time with school-friends, and very soon after I left school I met Simon, my husband, the man on the curious sofa.

Gangs of us went on expeditions at dawn to admire out-of-the-way bits of railway stations. Simon may not have been the first to do this but he did it because he enjoyed such things – has never done anything for any other reason I think, and all he does he does with his whole heart. Now that he is successful and has a hand in setting the fashion, people often forget this about him, but it is true.

Our party was a bit shrill however, perhaps to impress Simon, becoming shriller as the porters and cleaners began to stare; and cups of tea in the porters' hidey-hole with nobody wanting us there but too polite to say so was neither friendly nor funny, but Simon and his friends (and I was one who am now his wife) made it seem so. Victoriana spread to the gossip-columns so we moved on to American pop singers, and even that now seems a million years ago. *Times* leaders are written about the Beatles whereas in those days it never mentioned anything later than George Robey. This is part of the filtering upwards of popular taste that has gone pretty far by now I think, but it had to happen and Simon was one of the people who brought this about, although he never thought of any taste but his own. (Leader of the Elvis cult, he continued to buy up vast Victorian paintings which nobody else wanted. Some of these he has now sold for big sums. It's odd how sometimes I cling to that – as though money is at least a form of reality.)

It was fun decorating this house. We went to Norfolk and Scotland and parts of Surrey being redeveloped and from houses about to be demolished we rescued fireplaces (this one for instance from a Moorish palazzo near Weybridge) and ornaments and painted panels and all sorts of overlooked objects. Then we had all the fuss of transporting these cumbersome trophies by railway, overcoming the objections of the various officials who tried to think of reasons for stopping us. It may all sound rather precious and perhaps it was, but there was a good contrast between the heavy, self-confident, over-decorated objects we lugged to London and the nervous, functional people we moved among.

I loved Simon for his insistence on it all. He never theorized like this, would laugh at me for doing so. But when you are not naturally sure of something, and you've married it, you have to think it out as best you can.

However – what could be more boring than the restlessness of the young and rich? If there were days when I could have taken a hammer to the simpering angel on the stairs and smashed the glass dome that protects the model of Balmoral made from sea-shells – behaved, in short, like a hysterical female, I'm convinced this happens to all wives at times, to all human beings. If I felt trapped, suddenly, as I looked in that evening, it was not by marriage, not by Simon, not by any mistaken choice (the one I made at eighteen was the only one I could have made) but in a way I can't explain by time itself; as though loyalty to the person I had been at eighteen was confusing the loyalty I owed to myself at twenty-four. Of course loyalty to other people came into it too, but distorting oneself for the sake of others is a kind of insult to them. However, I certainly didn't believe my problem would necessarily be solved by a change of husband (or décor). My life wasn't asking for another life to feed on but for an opportunity, itself, to be a bit more alive. Like everyone else I wanted things to be more important than they seemed to have become, and, like nearly everyone else, I was more than a little scared when I thought how important, probably, they were.

So when I met Colm it never occurred to me that he would be any sort of answer. Nor was he – except in a wider sense than I knew anything about at the time. Let me try and explain – quickly, because I ought to get on with the story, which is a love story, and also, of course, a story about people. But as I've been writing it down (leaving this bit till the last) I've become more and more certain that what I am really trying to describe is not so much a love between two people, or even *people* at all, but the way it sometimes seemed there was an unbreakable thread, nearly graspable, that ran through the centre of it all. Details, events, personalities are the medium we bobbed about in, nearer and further away from that still, centre line. When we get nearest to it (which doesn't happen often) the less important individualities become. They flake away as we approach a life that was there before we were born and will be there when we are dead. It's not indifferent – it's waiting for us to see it. In spite of everything, *everything*, that happens to us and to others, it is still quietly waiting, like – this is what I wanted to describe – like an astonishing promise of the permanent existence of joy . . .

But there is a story of course, and it properly begins when I met Colm at a party given by an old school-friend of mine.

Dawn keeps up with me because she thinks Simon might introduce her to what she calls interesting people. I don't mind this.

I only noticed Colm because he was talking, or rather listening, to Dawn with an expression of such good-natured attention I could see her beginning to doubt whether he was worth talking to, she kept looking over his shoulder, saw me and called out:

'Trixie!' (I don't like being called Trixie – my name is Beatrix.) 'Trust you and Simon to be late. Popular beasts! This is –'

'Colm Treacey,' he said quietly, as though saving her the trouble. Dawn noticed something at the other end of the room, and rushed off. He just looked at me. I asked him if he knew Dawn well because I was disconcerted by his silence and his stare. His eyes were strange, bowl shaped, the lids at the top were almost straight, and I noticed his voice, low, without any strain in it. We talked a little, about nothing much.

It was clear that he liked women, I mean really liked them, which is rarer than one might hope. He knew Simon and knew I was married and he gave me the impression that he didn't regard me as out of the running for that reason. I don't know why. I wasn't on that track at all. But the conversation seemed to get a little out of hand without anything special being said – this is partly because he listened and looked at me as though I was really there, which doesn't happen very often between people.

Dawn arrived to break us up. I saw him later talking to another girl much more freely than he'd talked to me, waving his arms, his hair over his forehead. I wondered how well he knew her. Then I lost sight of him altogether.

I left the party before Simon because some people we knew had bought a picture they wanted to show me. When I got home Simon was in bed. I went and had a bath and afterwards I looked at myself in the long mirror in the bathroom. I'm larger than I would like but I thought Colm Treacey might like to see me like that, which was a new feeling. It didn't shock me. I didn't think about it. I got into bed beside Simon, who told me about a piece he was writing for the Third Programme on Vampires (was it? I know he made me laugh) and I wondered if anything would come of this evening and decided probably not, and just as well, and fell asleep.

For a little while, in what follows, I shall have to invent. I don't mind this because we do invent people we know. We can't be with them all the time, we make them up from things they say and from things we notice. They play their parts in our heads. I'll begin with Colm at his office. I never saw him there, but he talked about it later. Then I'll go on to Mr Findus and Margaret. They, and several other people, have their part in the story.

2

He put down his Biro, yawned, and looked at the stubs of cigarettes disintegrating in the slopped saucer of his office tea, remembering its taste on his furred tongue. What did they put in it? Even tea didn't taste like itself in this building. And Findus was always saying 'Ah! ... *Tea*.' with what sounded like genuine pleasure. He laughed, and regretted it. The combination of that tea and too many cigarettes had hung the passages in his head with charred cobwebs.

'Miss Florentine ...'

The door between their two little rooms always stood ajar, and he had grown more or less accustomed during the two years he had been in this place to yawning, scratching, laughing, making digestive noises, even sleeping, in the presence (invisible) of someone whose Christian name he knew but which she did not encourage him to use. She, on the other hand, when not actually typing, made no sound at all. King Chronos seemed to ride her very lightly. She emerged as fresh at five-thirty as she arrived (always before he did) in the morning. A day gone forever in her young life and never a tremor of fear.

She appeared.

'Timor mortis conturbat me,' Colm said, not hopefully. She never responded out of character.

'Have you finished the article then?' She smiled, beautifully, but who for? Who in God's name had taught her to be this way? What obscure revenge was being worked out on the whole male sex by the lady-teachers in a thousand secretarial schools?

'Yes. Get it off tomorrow morning will you? ... It's rubbish,' he added quietly; he could never bring himself entirely to give up hope.

'Pardon?'

'Nothing.'

Why had Fate chosen to plonk him in the middle of this particular, particularly wrong-headed, détente in the relation between the sexes? Women were the equals of men *all right*! But what was so equal about being anonymous?

'You look very nice today.' There was something appalling about nothing whatsoever happening between two human beings.

'Thank you.' She plucked at the horizontal frills that ran down the front of her blouse and gazed objectively at her considerable bosom. 'C. and A.' She might have been talking to another girl in the washroom.

'Go away. You're driving me mad with lust and indecision.' That was true and dishonest, because he knew she would never believe it. Was it him? Did he appear as grey to her as this building made him feel? Ah, vanity –

'... if you have time to see him.'

'What?'

'Mr Findus. He would like to see you.'

'Would he, bejasus.' God not the comic-Irish thing as well! This girl put him out of kilter. 'Does he want me to go down?'

'No. He said he'd come up when you'd finished. Shall I tell him?'

'Yes, do. And tomorrow, when you've finished that – knock off early if you want to.'

She laughed gaily. 'What, with all the overflow from the pool to cope with?'

'Are you a plumber as well then?'

'Typing pool.' Unsmiling.

'Ah.'

She tip-tapped away to her invisible corner with his absurd article like a laundress with his laundry. Bored with her, with himself, he grunted and swung his head from side to side, trying to make the last few moments go spinning towards the cream-painted walls, as though they were a heavy insect that had landed in his hair.

What did Findus want?

He examined his conscience, but soon gave up. He would have sacked himself long ago.

Findus he loved, that old tweedy mole, burrowing privately among his tasks on the floor below – Cultural Chief of this whole echoing Institute; he had the air of a man who knew when he had it made, which was what Colm liked about him. He had unexpected enthusiasms too, for the jazzier kinds of Beat poetry among other things; was full of surprising, gamey flavours, like a very old Chinese egg.

'There you are!' Findus, putting his large round face through Miss Florentine's door (the only entrance to Colm's room) sounding surprised. He always did. 'Not great thoughts I hope?'

'No. I was expecting you.'

'Heh! We'll let that pass.' He carefully closed the connecting-door behind him. 'Excellent girl that,' he whispered, his head slightly thrown back as though sniffing Colm with his eyes. He was like something out of *The Wind in the Willows*.

'Yes,' said Colm. Findus could become embarrassing on the subject of women. It was his idea of camaraderie. 'Let me clear this chair for you.'

'No, no. I'd prefer to pace, thank you. At this time of the afternoon I find sitting down conducive to – ah – contemplation – heh? Although we're absolutely inundated downstairs, of course.' The pool overflowing again? 'As you are too I'm sure.'

'Well I wouldn't say –'

'Quite. Little do They know how They drive us – we who bear the burden of the heat of the day.'

Findus creaked to the window in his shining brown boots and stared for a moment through the glass at a miniature cactus that had lain on its side, markedly dead, gathering soot on the outside sill for as long as Colm had been there.

'"I didn't get much sleep last night thinking about underwear."'

'I'm sorry to hear that.'

Colm saw his role as straight-man to the other's Potty Professor.

'Ferlinghetti. Do you know it?

Women's underwear holds things up.
Men's underwear holds things down.

'Splendid humorous directness, something we have lost. Aren't we all obsessed with underwear? Those photographs near the moving stairway in the Underground. These mini-skirts inviting the eye up vanishing vistas. Crammed full of unpurged images we return, red-rimmed, to our desks. Eunuchs of the eye, each of us nursing a quiverful of unsatisfied desires. There is no health in us, my dear Colm!' Findus turned towards him the shining cheeks and clear blue eyes of an entirely self-contented man. 'We shrivel!'

Colm yawned, too widely, and shook his head while he got his jaw under control, trying to suggest that his yawn was intended as visual corroboration of the shrivelling concept. Findus sighed and fumbled in the pocket of his sagging green tweed suit, producing an old pipe and matches, still gazing appreciatively at the cactus.

'My apple trees have capsid bugs,' the pipe delved deep into striped pouch (college colours?), the fingers, invisible, manipulating: 'And my dear wife is by no means well.'

Again Colm tried to imagine a Mrs Findus. Cardiganed on the sofa, sitting-room curtains partly drawn, the returned Findus peering out of the window, filling his pipe, lamenting as always the dreadful new bungalow across the way. But it was always Findus he saw, not his wife. And what of the underwear that was holding Findus down, under the browning green tweed? There was a kind of uniform, he thought, for dons, dons manqués, and BBC producers of the Findus generation: a shirt of some woollen stuff, dun-coloured and obtrusively limp of collar, a unicoloured tie, also of wool, and then the sad cascade of tweed, vaguely urinous about the fly, giving the impression that, off, it would leak old, spent gases.

'I feel, my dear Colm, that you need some assistance.' He was watching him anxiously.

'Why?'

He appeared to come to a decision. 'May I sit down?' He settled himself and leaned forward. 'You are overworked.'

'Oh,' said Colm.

Findus sighed with relief, took off his spectacles, breathed on them and began vigorously to polish them with his tie. His eyes looked small and unprotected.

'Parkinson's Law. The assistant you so badly need would swell the size of your establishment. With a larger establishment we all automatically move up a peg in the wage-scale. *But,*' he went on quickly, although Colm showed no signs of interrupting, 'we can also give ourselves the kind of leisure we need for our kind of work. If we asked for it we would be laughed at. If we do not complain of overwork we will be considered *under*worked. He who is underworked is soon redundant. There is a kind of language in these matters that it is foolish not to learn.' He got up and stared into the dank cell of the courtyard, his pipe still unlit. 'Do you know what they did the day war broke out? Closed the British Museum and the National Gallery. Not to move the things inside. Just to stop us going in. A kind of reflex action: enough of such fripperies, time now for Real Life.

'This place,' he waved his arm vaguely, 'is not much. We are not much, but we have the right to live; as necessary as many, more so than some.' He paused. 'Colm – in early days man set forth from his cave armed only with a club and his superior cunning. The situation is unchanged. We who have chosen neither silence nor exile have need, the more so, for that last quality.'

How was it possible not to love this splendid old twister? And yet ... Colm felt the cobwebs begin to hang not only inside his head but outside as well, over his face and clothes. What was emanating benevolently, even wisely, from the roly-poly uncle now contentedly screening himself with smoke, was the smell of twenty more years of disappointment than he had yet had to endure. He was not ready for the Findus survival-kit.

'... and Margaret needs a holiday. Frankly these improvements in our office arrangements will make that financially possible.'

Colm gave a prolonged, end-of-conversation yawn. There were dangers in allowing oneself to become too depressed by Findus, who was himself, after his little speech, delighted by the contemplation of his own honesty. He qualified the yawn by a friendly, end-of-the-working-day stretch.

'I look forward to your report then,' said Findus, and Norman Pinswell, never far from Charles on any occasion, poked his nearly naked scalp round the door.

'Ah ! Charles.'

He carried his usual sheaf of papers never venturing into the corridors without it, made the usual apologies, and the two older men, equally delighted to be together again, went off, clucking.

Colm had never been able to discover what Pinswell actually did. He and Findus had interconnecting rooms, impressively tome-lined, the door between them always open; and from Pinswell's cluttered and enormous desk (behind which could just be discerned the diminutive Pinswell, rapt, forehead in left palm, right hand in the act of composition), crept a slow tide of biographies and monographs on subjects always quite outstandingly dull. These were neither scholarly nor popular, escaping the attention of those who really knew the subject and the attention of everybody else as well. As a result they were always respectfully reviewed: 'A study of some of the lesser personalities involved in the Battle of Preston invaluable to all students of the subject – lucidly and elegantly written', the adjectives revealing that the reviewer had never got past the blurb. In this way he had become quite widely known. What he did for the organization that employed him nobody (and this was a masterpiece of the Findus technique) had remembered to ask for fifteen years.

This place was a narrow interstice into which the Pinswells crawled. And the Treaceys?

The thing about biting the hand that fed, the thing about help in general ... it was never quite the kind of help required. And there was a grotesque element; Colm found more and more that he was allowing Findus to help him in order to help Findus, it made the old boy so happy. So he took the money and didn't really do the job – all in the cause of Art presumably. But how was that? He hadn't written a note of music for five weeks. Something dismal was creeping into him, like damp. He yawned; he didn't really believe that, but it was time to go home anyway.

He climbed down the uncarpeted concrete stairs behind a girl of normal proportions who had encased her behind in a taut rebarbative drum. In the interests of chastity this would have made sense, but her intention was so clearly otherwise and she was so entirely mistaken that Colm had one of his frequent spasms of despair.

He emerged into the breathed-out, fumed-up, fag-end of an early spring day. The clouds over Oxford Street were turning a thunderous grey and dark-blue and black, sharply edged with orange and daffodil yellow; an apocalypse of a sky. People just out from work, faces briefly gilded by the clear, pre-rain, evening light, were beginning to hurry as the first large drops briefly gave the pavement the appearance of being cobbled. Colm, an *Evening Standard* over his head, took refuge in a doorway.

He admitted to himself that the last thing he wanted to do was go home. There he would have to sit down at his piano and work. It was becoming very difficult to do this after a day at the office; something seemed to die in him which took progressively longer to revive.

He stared through the rain-slowed track to the other side of the street at the brightly lit windows of Imhof's, filled with blown-up photographs of virtuosi, pyramids and lakes of coloured record-sleeves, and behind them in the shop all the intricate tempting machines, shining like toys, for the reproduction of their sounds. One window was entirely given over to the works of a young composer, not much older than himself, for whose work he felt less than admiration.

He thought of his room. When he closed the door behind him these days the things he had left behind in the morning, his dirty cornflakes bowl on the floor, the single whisky glass of the previous night, sticky inside, the open book, also on the floor, gave out no welcoming resonance but a tingling, ringing noise of fever, as though bunched, balancing, ready to explode. If there was more than one whisky glass from the previous night, a greater confusion than usual in the bed, that was, if anything, worse.

He didn't weep crocodile tears over an aloneness he had chosen. But as he sat at his piano, dryly adding one phrase to another, he could not understand why the pool of music he knew was buried inside him was these days so difficult to tap; or why he wanted to reach it at all. Was it any more than a fear of mediocrity and a fear of his own death?

Hell, why *should* it be more than that!

The weather had cleared now, the clouds that had looked thick enough to dent the nose of an aeroplane had disappeared and the sky was a lingering evening green. Colm remembered he would not have to do battle with himself tonight after all – he was going out. Dropping his sodden evening paper into a litter-box, he went to a kiosk and telephoned Derek. Derek was going too; they could eat together beforehand.

Charles Findus, mackintoshed, his countryman's trilby corrugated of brim and several shades darker from the rain, went into his favourite horticultural shop on his way home and chose a potted plant for his wife.

Holborn was full of shops that he had made his favourite for this and that. He ferreted for touches of individuality with infinite patience, discovering after years what one shop, café or pub did better than its neighbours or at least less badly and bad-temperedly. It was necessary to him, this creation of the illusion of a village. He wandered through the piece of the city he had made personal to himself, not as squire, or vicar, not as a genuine inhabitant at all (he admitted) but as a kind of ageing eccentric curator, here exchanging a greeting, there inhaling old familiar fragrances. Of course, sometimes it happened to him, more and more of late, that he would return to some corner not visited for months, checking his landmarks as he went, only to find himself blinking up at a tall shine of glass and concrete. Perhaps he had mistaken his way? Then he would understand, with a quick suck of fear, that it was not he who was lost but the way itself. If there were shop-fronts in the new façade he would quickly gird himself, cross the road, and in the pile-carpeted chainstore tobacconist (say) stand companionably stuffing his pipe and chatting while the assistants stared and shuffled. He would not be abashed. What happiness he had managed to wrest from life had come from just this insistance that life really was as he felt it should be, not the smooth cold surface that more and more it pretended to present.

But there were days when he was overcome and his courage failed. There was the time when he went to an erstwhile favourite pub, neglected of late, and found a cloud of dust and a hole in the ground filled with clawing machines; there was something about those machines, indifferent and scaly, that frightened him. The last to fall (he had been in time to see it) were the brown porcelain tiles of the hideous, ludicrous and utterly personal doorway, with a number denoting the sequence of execution written with a finger in its dust. They had not been halcyon nights passed on those boards where the hole now was: nothing out of the ordinary. But the place had been for humans and human-sized even in its vulgarly grandiose waste of space; and what would go up in its place would be both smaller than human and infinitely too large. It was as though what small message he wished to share with his fellow-men was being whirled through dusty corridors of hostile space, unheard, unheeded, and he was an old, failed relic hung with outmoded clothes and of no account at all. He knew he was that as well, but to be made to feel *only* that was the Devil himself.

The affair of the plant, however, had been satisfactory. The girl had seemed to have sufficient time to allow the purchase to be conducted as it should be, with a proper beginning, middle and end. And the cyclamen would not too greatly have shocked Marvell's Mower, its colour and size still owed more to nature than to the improvements and enforcement of man. It *had* been forced alas, and of course, (and therefore it would not last).

He relished the thought of Margaret's face when he gave it to her. He was always filled with wonder at the attachment the best women showed to the tangible. Twenty-five years of his love evidenced this evening, for Margaret, by an undistinguished potted plant that she could take from him and hold, pleased as a girl. He knew that today she would have had bad news and that she would forget it as soon as she saw, clear in his hands, that for five minutes during the day he had thought of her.

From Waterloo Station the journey was crowded, the rush as steaming as usual, but he had never been able to resent the multiplication of his fellow human beings. No more than anyone else did he enjoy being pushed, but short of the capital sum that he always wished he had (for with money in any economy you can buy yourself space and thus give your life the necessary appearance of uniqueness), he was glad to take part in the rhythm of a working city. His Communism of the 'thirties had given way, slowly, ever since the Nazi-Soviet pact (although during the war he had once again hoped), to what he privately termed 'a Marxist Individualism'. Although he despised present Western society, which seemed to him suicidal, he was aware of its advantages for such as he, and of the horrors within it he might equally have undergone. A Charles Findus in digs, jobless, humoured by barmaids, 'with pee-stains on his underwear' (as his favourite, Gregory Corso, had put it) – he had escaped that so far. The slender props of his position and his adequate salary allowed him to cherish his sense of failure like a private vice, whereas it might have swept over him in a bitter, salt wave. For this he was grateful.

No – as for people, the more the merrier, why not? He could not help, nevertheless, regretting the houses that had sprung up all along his walk from the station to where he lived. How could one not regret the buttercup meadows of the immediately post-war years? (He quickly checked – yes, there really *had* been buttercup meadows.) And was it not strange, the way laburnum in bloom, so startlingly yellow on the fringe of a green wood, should bear such a weepy, funeral-parlour air, caught between gate and privet hedge?

A slow flush began to rise in his cheeks....

As he had turned the corner past the pub (Victorian, early, simple and not at all bad) into the fifty yards or so of street that still retained some of their original character, he saw that outside the pub, on a narrow uneven strip of pavement, there had been set shiny tin tables with a hole in the centre and into the holes were stuck huge umbrellas, brightly coloured in sections, with the word *Cinzano* on a kind of frill round the brim. These had the effect, while looking completely out of place themselves, of making everything around them look equally inappropriate. With a stroke of genius that Charles was daily finding it easier to regard as Satanic, they rendered silly and meaningless the last that was old as well as good about the place where he lived.

But what, he tried to comfort himself, would Gregory Corso make of it, or some of the others? They helped him. Just as Auden had helped him and, before that, Rupert Brooke (about whom he remained unrepentant): they gave a shape to his reactions. They (his favourite poets nowadays) had taken upon themselves the contemporary urban world of garishness and outrage, setting up shop in the middle of it; and there they sang with a stridence that was appropriate and infinitely better than flight. Regarding the tables, which had for the moment grown a look of barbarous innocence, he firmly pushed open the door of the pub.

It was not long after opening time and there was the usual sense of waiting ashtrays, the clock preternaturally loud, the publican newly scrubbed and slit-eyed after his siesta.

There was also the inevitable solitary drinker talking quietly to the publican, hunched on a stool. Romantic music from which all erotic content had been filleted, the only small meaning it had ever possessed, emanated from somewhere on the wall, Charles suspected from behind a burnished warming-pan.

'Quite the stranger!' The publican's voice, pitched at a volume more suitable for closing time, made the leaded panes rattle. This man, a retired Wing Commander or some such thing, greeted all members of the middle class with a cordiality that seemed to force them and himself into some kind of conspiracy. He also had a wife of startling gentility who occasionally pulled pints in the Public Bar with an air of one delivering gruel to the poor. To Charles' depression she was rather popular with her customers.

He smiled, hoped blandly. Perhaps a tentative bearing witness?

'Those tables ...'

The publican groaned and held up his hand.

'Don't, my dear old man! They've been on order for six months and they arrived this morning with the wrong-sized poles for the umbrellas! They just don't *care* any more!' This last was addressed to the solitary drinker, who snorted on cue:

'I hear the dockers are at it again.'

'I know what I'd do to 'em.'

Charles tried once more. 'A bit bright aren't they?'

'. . . I'm sorry, old man?'

'The tables.'

'Touch of the Continentals eh? Ha-hargh!' His laugh developed into a tearing coughing fit that he seemed to enjoy. 'Aaargh!' he gasped, and wiped his mouth as though polishing it. 'Well, what can I do you for?'

Charles surveyed the collection of small plastic barrels that lined the front of the bar, each with a famous name attached – *Worthington E*, *Bass*, and so on. From them, he knew, would issue gaseous imitations of their old selves tasting, identically, of squid.

'You haven't any ordinary bitter from the wood, have you?'

'Bit late in the day for that, old man. Keg?'

Didn't the fellow ever drink the stuff himself?

'I'll have a half then.'

'Of which one?'

'How many have you?'

'Five.'

'I'll have a half of the cheapest.'

'And the best of British,' said the landlord, 'a half of old and nasty coming up.' It came up, or rather down, out of a little tap immediately and with a regimented froth; instant beer.

'Thank you.'

'A very great pleasure,' yelled the landlord and turned with emphasis to resume his conversation with the solitary drinker.

Charles took himself and his drink to join Margaret's potted plant at a formica-topped table. The trouble with all our civilizations, he decided while he crossed, Marxist and Capitalist alike, was too much obedience. Impotence in the face of monopoly and centralization. Made people want to break things. Made some people, mostly young, do just that.

A tall man of indefinite appearance burst through the door and threw an evening paper on the bar, clapping a bowler hat beside it with a small hollow explosion. 'That's *it*!' he said, 'If this lot stay in, I'm off!' The publican wordlessly poured a pint and pushed it across to him. 'Where's the incentive in this country? Tell me.'

'I needed that!' This last was gasped on emergence from the

pint pot. He seemed actually to enjoy the stuff, Charles saw with interest. 'What'll you have?'

'Nothing just now, thanks,' said the landlord. 'Going easy for a bit.' Here he tapped his stomach with affection before turning to cough enormously over a small piece of shrivelled lemon on a saucer. Later in the evening he would be saying 'Ice? Lemon?' to those who ordered gins and tonics with the air of a man obsessively generous with his time and his fruit. This spasm prolonged itself and he appeared to relish the indisputably male sound of it. 'Aaargh shoo!' he said finally into a huge coloured handkerchief, his eyes streaming.

'How many is it now, George?' said the solitary drinker respectfully.

'Sixty a day,' said the landlord, lighting another of the sixty as though playing Russian roulette.

Charles sighed again over his terrible drink. Grey wavelets of depression scurfed over the carpet towards his toes. There came a time when observation, endurance, became merely masochistic. He got up.

'Have you any half-bottles of Scotch?'

'With the greatest of pleasure! Which do you fancy?'

As Charles had known he would, the landlord had only one sort of whisky in half-bottles and that was his least favourite. Always only the illusion of a choice. It was wrapped carefully in white tissue paper as though an obscene object and, putting it in his pocket, leaving his beer, Charles collected his plant and went out into a now magnificent evening.

The sun had moved away from the umbrellas and these looked almost apologetic in the cooling shadow. Soon there would be a heavy smell of roses from the small gardens that lined the road. Too many roses; rose-trees carefully tethered, bushes pruned and propped, roses climbing over the new sore brick and round the metal window-frames, each set in a mound of carefully mixed and artificial soil containing all the vitamins, and cut into beds cuticle-shaped or circular, oblong or triangle, with tiny causeways of grass between, and the roses, so well fed, would grow in such profusion and to such size and colour that the gardens looked like fruit sundaes, half-conscious over-conciliation to the countryside these necessary houses had despoiled. But their scent would be pleasant on the road, mixing with the smell of tar and motor cars.

The economy-sized gables of the Edwardian Midland Bank still caught the last rays of the sun and the huge chestnut in the corner of the car park (spared by what unknown soldier?) gave back to the sun a soft green shine from its leaves just beginning to unfurl, while in its centre small blue shadows moved privately.

'Is that you, Charles?'

'Hang on a minute, darling. I'll just put away my things.'

Charles liked to savour his homecoming, wait a moment for the day to slough off and for the next part of it to begin. He had never been able to train Margaret; she always heard him first. He changed his jacket, loosened his tie and put on some more comfortable shoes, sitting in the little dark hall and wondered (as he often did, there were fixed points in his mental life to which he returned) at the chance that had allowed him, after all these years, to say 'darling' like that and mean it. He straightened from tying his shoes and was immediately engulfed in the folds and smells of his old rubber mackintosh. He was not a glamorous man, not even a particularly interesting one. What had made Margaret seek him out and, what was more marvellous still, remain? He clasped the potted plant and went in to her.

Colm had imagined Mrs Findus very well, so far as such imaginings can go. She was indeed lying on a sofa, cardiganed. The curtains were half-drawn over the windows, and outside, when they had first moved here, there had indeed been the famous meadows. What he could not have guessed was her beauty.

She had dark yellow hair, fairly long, and drawn back softly across her forehead; it was still the hair of a young girl, and the powder of grey on it, or rather the slight loss of colour, seemed only to give it a pinky depth. Youthful hair against ageing skin can present a grotesque effect, but her extraordinary pallor and her large violet eyes made her look neither more nor less than her age, as though touched by time precisely, her beauty preserved not by chance but by the kind of person she was. She stirred delightedly at the sight of the plant.

'Oh, Charles! How sweet you are...'

She took it and looked at it and then up at him and in fact behaved, to his pleasure, just as he had known she would. He busied himself unwrapping the half bottle of whisky, finding tumblers.

'What news?' he said, his back to her.

'Oh – the usual. D'you think I could have some water with it? Quite a lot.' She continued talking to him as he went to the tap in the kitchen. 'You know Woodburn. I don't think he actually used the phrase "dickie ticker", but I'm always expecting him to.'

The discovery of her bad heart about two years before, although frightening them both and giving Margaret sometimes fearful stabs of pain, had long ago come to be considered as a sort of third party between them. There had in fact been a child, a son, whom Charles had never much liked and whom Margaret had regarded with mild affectionate wonder. He had died in early manhood after a brief illness, and for Charles it was another kind of wonder that a human life could have had so little significance to those presumably closest to it – or to anyone else.

As for Margaret's heart, her visits to the specialist were become formalities merely, shadowed by the anxiety that this time he might feel compelled to pronounce her sentence, even put a term to her life. This time, thank God, it clearly had not happened, but Charles could tell that she had learned from the doctor's silence that there was certainly no improvement.

'I could kiss Woodburn when he says "No excitement". It's like being given a licence to dream. Tell me you don't think I'm just lazy.'

'A truly lazy person can't bring himself to do what he wants, as a result he's the most irritating company. Whereas you don't want to do anything, the most restful person I know.'

Margaret laughed. 'In that case I shall cook your supper.' She carefully put the flap of the book she had been reading to mark her place and folded back the rug from her legs. Charles watched her precise movements and the way her eyes moved from distance to nearness with an exactness that he loved. It was as though her glance had the capacity to receive from everything it rested on all the inwardness that thing had. She possessed, more than anyone Charles had ever known, the poetic sensibility and yet she had no talent or need for creativity. She had the sense of direction of a bird calmly negotiating invisible pockets of air. She was her own expression. She was so perfectly ordinary and yet so unlike what a human being ought to be that Charles privately considered her a miracle and the thought made him uneasy. Her existence was his joy; the implications of her existence were a puzzle to him.

He turned his head sideways to read the title of the book she had been reading which she had put on the floor: *King of Clay*. The life of Sir Oliver Wynstone, Potter Extraordinary. By Norman Pinswell.

'Any good?' he called.

'Suppose so. It's just that Sir Oliver Thingummy isn't a very interesting man.'

'Worth doing?'

'Oh yes.'

Well, he reflected, it was probably true; in the tiny scope of patronage that he wielded he could not demand that his single goose should be a swan. Little men at work, although perhaps not architects, could be thought of as stone-masons. But certainly it was a long time since he had picked up one of his friend's books hopefully.

'He has a new girl-friend.' Charles followed her into the kitchen. 'I can always tell. He starts having little murmured conversations into the telephone.'

'Have you met her?'

'Her existence has not yet been admitted. I hope she is an improvement on the Finn.'

'Where *does* he find them?'

'The English Speaking Club I think. And the less of it they speak the better.'

'They always seem so physically – voracious. And Norman is so...'

'He may be a tiger.'

Margaret giggled and concentrated on her stove. Charles turned her towards him and put his finger-tips gently on her heart feeling it faintly move. Her hands, wet from preparing vegetables, went over his shoulders and she held his neck between her wrists, his head of thinning hair and thinning teeth, foolishly bespectacled. There was no more promise in him now, nothing to be hoped for. Still, this creature was contented with him. Well – it was one of the comforts of middle age – you settled into your own size, however small, and it was clear that still suited Margaret.

He brushed his cheek against hers and said 'Ten minutes?' and she said 'Not more', and he went upstairs to wash.

He was contented. And yet.... What was it in the heart and in the body that craved for stronger meat, for some kind of outrage, joy, pain? It was as if one's better part, and one's good fortune, could only exist uneasily without a glimpse acknowledging their darker counterpart. He stood by the little table in his room and took from the back of a drawer a small packet of photographs. These he had bought one day in Soho from a breezy young man who stood in a shop surrounded by boxes of such things. The photographs were of five naked people, three girls and two men, in complicated sexual contact on a crumpled bed. He looked at them with mild stirrings of an interest difficult to define simply as lust (or was it perhaps that rarity, simple lust?) and also he looked at them with affection. He particularly loved the details. One of the men, flat on his back, his feet towards the spectator, was still wearing socks. The clock on the sideboard (the room looked like a bed-sitter) said ten to one, and in the corner of one of the photographs, lying on the floor, was an empty bottle of whisky – Ballantine's, he could just make out. One girl he was fond of because she was the only one, eyes half-shut, who seemed to be enjoying what she did and what was done to her. The others were for the most part blank-faced, even lost-looking, as they strove acrobatically to reach some relevant portion of another. What did they think they were doing? Why did he wish to look at them doing it? He would never take part in such an occasion and he was pretty sure he did not want to. Norman, for example, would never need such surrogates. He smiled as he thought of Norman and his series of melancholy foreign students. Did he, Charles, simply need to have one guilty secret from Margaret? If in fact she knew, would she do anything but laugh? She called out to him to come downstairs for supper. He shuffled the photographs together, pushed them again to the back of the drawer and started to go down the stairs, his mind full of a last impression of naked limbs and dark, secret hair.

3

A week or two previously Colm had received an invitation on an expensive card – Dawn Slope requested the pleasure of his company to meet her brother Edward and to celebrate the publication of his collection of poems *LSD* – (this, he deduced after some puzzling, was the title of the book). He thought no more about it, having heard of neither of them, until he discovered that Derek would be there, that indefatigable pursuer of the off-chance, which indicated the likelihood of girls. Colm rang him from the telephone box and they arranged to meet.

Derek was an old friend, unmarried, and this gave him importance among the diminished number of Colm's footloose acquaintance. Colm used him as a kind of thinking-machine on which he tested his own unconscious assumptions. Derek's quiet 'Why?' made him aware of the sludge of old negatives and imperatives unsifted at the bottom of his head. This was interesting. So were some of Derek's own unconscious assumptions, although more rationally based. For some years now he had been busy (very busy, the amount of energy required was prodigious) narrowing his life down to a basis of reason. This had reached tangible rock-bottom at sex and stayed there. Colm considered that all such narrowing down was bound to reach such an apparent bottom – only a layer over the caverns of ultimate cannibalism. Derek was a rationalist, however, and detested violence; was, in fact, much less than reasonable on the subject.

He was literary editor of one of the highbrow weeklies, published an occasional, successful critical work which caused in Colm an impatience he could only salve with laughter. But these activities were merely a source of subsidy for his tom-cat private life. (Colm found nothing that was less than sensible in the behaviour of tom-cats.)

He was eating with Derek in an hour and there was no point in going home. He walked in the direction of St James's Park, the crowd mostly sluicing into Charing Cross. He negotiated the swirling emptiness of Trafalgar Square where people protested and jumped in the fountains on New Year's Eve, the television cameras waiting, the revellers obediently disobedient, the dripping policemen extracting them, just that satisfactory bit too roughly. Cyprus, Suez – you name them, he'd been there, protesting with the rest. What he remembered now was a damp Sunday afternoon, waiting for a friend, half-watching a meeting of some kind. There was a handful of spectators, idle as himself, feeding the pigeons, the cinemas were not yet open. The speech the man was making was the stuff of all speeches, justice for the workers, a new Britain: 'And now – it is my great pleasure to introduce the next speaker – my friend, your friend – that well-known Anti-Semite from East Finchley – Les Parkinson!' Colm laughed, for it was funny. Not elsewhere, a few years before. But that was in another country and besides ... there was never anything to be ashamed of in laughing.

No more heady indignations, blaming Them. Now it was more difficult to love 'the Beings by your own Fireside'. Big things from little acorns grew, not the other way about.

He stood for a moment in front of the memorial to the Royal Artillery dead of the South African War, individual names set in letters of bronze, a personal attention for which we no longer have room.

The park – the trees were just coming out – was full of lovers on the grass and people watching them and other people watching the water birds. The weight of the surrounding buildings gave it an apologetic air like a poor relation dolled-up; its prettiness tried too hard.

Seven magnificent pelicans, in flotilla formation, chose that moment to steam grandly down the little lake in search of fish. They dipped their beaks in unison and brought them out again almost together, before sweeping on. They were a wonderful whitey-pink colour and their plumage had a shaggy, careless and dashing looseness like the black plumes in a Bersaglieri hat. Not for them the urban quarrelsomeness of the sleek duck. Far from their Africa they made the best of a bad job, together, with indifference and pride. But even they, he noticed, needed the permission of science and the authorities to survive. A constant spray of oxygenated water was directed into the lake. The air of the town was making the water unfit for fish, the food for the pelican. Poor town. Poor fish.

Colm pushed the opened box of tipped Woodbines across the café table. He always carried one box of fifty open and another, unopened, in his pocket. He was the only man Derek knew who never ran out of cigarettes however small the hour of the morning. However, Derek waved them away, preferring his own at this stage.

'Who was that lady I saw you with last night?' said Colm, lighting another one.

'When?'

Derek's lack of memory, Colm privately considered, amounted almost to insanity. He seemed only able to remember what immediately concerned his appetites; that, and almost everything he had learned at school. Around these two areas of sharply focused light were static pools of voluntary amnesia. He tried again.

'I saw you last night. We waved. You were with a girl. Who was she?'

Derek concentrated and then his face cleared to the exact degree of frankness he considered the question to merit. If anything he enjoyed the constant unmalicious probings that Colm went in for. In his attempts to answer them over the years he had been astonished to discover that he had accumulated something he considered beyond his range (or anyonc else's) – a very nearly coherent point of view. In return he enjoyed shoving at the patterns that Colm tried to find in his own life. Colm was always holding his experience up to the light and turning it round. Derek tried to knock it out of his hand, leave him groping, to show him you couldn't stop and consider, all you could do was move.

'Her name was Susan Woodthorpe and I met her last night at a party.'

'And were you successful?' There was no prurience in Colm's question. This was for the record.

'No. But that didn't matter.' Derek let his eyes move round the gloomy taxi-drivers' caff Colm had insisted they come to. Perhaps it was because he smoked so many cigarettes that he cared so little about food?

The pretty, fat daughter of the Italian proprietor stood by their table. Colm gave his order.

'Eggs, chips, bacon and a tea. Oh – and some bread and butter please. You?'

Derek was studying the card fixed under the glass of the table. 'Good Lord!' he said, 'Roast duck and green peas only three and six! That's fantastic.... I'll have that.'

Colm sighed. His advice had not been sought. He had learned, with Derek, not to offer it.

'It was just that you looked so... eager when I saw you.'

'She was a very sweet girl.'

Colm tried to remember her face. All he could see was two long streaks of fair-coloured hair almost concealing a well-shaped but nondescript quota of eyes, nose and mouth. And Derek, fifteen years her senior, leaning forward, his eyes enlarged with the effort to enthral, while she stared carefully in front of her. He was interested in his own reaction to the sight, the wave of fatigue that had flowed through him.

Their food arrived; his predictably reasonable, Derek's, also predictably, a taut blue-grey carcase and a pile of peas dyed bright green.

Colm made himself giddy remembering that vacant considering face. Good luck to her, but what had she to do with Derek? And if she was not as he imagined she would then be an individual of such value that there were only two courses open: flight or love. With the latter Derek was certainly not concerned.

'Where do you find the energy to shove through all that predictable brushwood?'

Derek thoughtfully examined his horrible plateful. He pushed it away as inedible and looked at Colm. Then he said carefully and seriously:

'It's the only interesting thing there is.'

With the spasm of depression that ran through Colm (oh God, was that true?) there was also one of affection. It was hope, he decided, that made Derek's world go round. A man who could believe in roast duck at three and six could believe in anything.

'Every girl is different in the way she makes love. Her reactions are different, that's what being alive is.'

Better to be tireless than tired.

'You want to be understood,' Derek said. 'We have to outgrow that one.'

True. But their attitudes to women, although they had roughly equivalent qualitative results, Derek moving towards coldness, Colm towards a frequently silly yearning, seemed to Colm similar in value but not in possibility. He felt he was playing the same game but for higher stakes, his gains and his losses might be greater because he risked and demanded more. Certainly his way was not 'better'. It was possible that Derek's acceptance of what he could get, of things-as-they-were, showed a humbler and more humane spirit. After all was it not he, Colm, who sought in sexual matters the cut-price duck, and Derek who sensibly settled for the fairly unspoilable egg and chips?

While they were in the café it had again rained and as they stood for a moment outside the air had a smell of damp carpets. The new leaves of the scrubby Pimlico plane-trees, briefly clean and briefly catching the last of the evening sun, asserted themselves, tinnily rustling, and there was an impression of washed, flashing windows. It was a pity, Colm thought, knowing that within two hours he would most certainly be drunk, that they had to go to an absurd party on such an evening, that London is an indoor city. Derek on the other hand, who would not be drunk in two hours, who would perhaps be adding a new page to his album, pointed like an old hunter in the direction they had to go, the scent of possibility, as it did every hunting evening, carrying to his nostrils. He hailed a taxi near the public lavatory, over which, Colm was telling him, the Council were thinking of putting a statue to Mozart.

Wanda, flattened against the wall, was being talked at by an elderly Irish poet who had his large palm on the wall just behind her head, imprisoning her. As he muttered down he stared with angry concentration between her breasts. Wanda, as befitted her middle-thirties, drew attention to the softness and whiteness of her upper parts while those below began to spread. She stared up at him.

Colm went towards her, circumnavigating the rapt wrist-shaking dancers, picked his way through the unbudging serious drinkers and nearly collided with the nose-high barrier of the poet's arm. He came round the open side.

'Piss off,' said the poet.

'All right,' said Colm and put his arm through Wanda's, withdrawing her gently from the burly right-angle of the poet through his open hypotenuse. She gave the poet one of her best smiles (they were always good) and was drawn away.

'He was telling me that everyone in this room is a phoney. True?'

'I should think so.'

'Who isn't then?'

'Him, I suppose.'

He led her round the edges to the shelter of a far wall, gathering another drink for both of them on the way. Wanda always asked questions, it was her way of finding out someone else's mood, all she ever asked was something to respond to.

'But I've heard how amusing he is.'

'People love to be insulted – makes them feel unstuffy. They don't really believe that anyone so obviously poor *can* insult them. He knows this and it makes him even more savage; i.e. more amusing.' Colm yawned. Wanda had a trick of making you explain things she already knew.

'You should have been nicer to him.'

'Professional un-phonies always loathe each other. You must have a monopoly, or self-doubt creeps in.'

'You're not a professional. You're just nice. Anyway, he wasn't insulting me – he was telling me about his mother.'

'Oh, the Irish!' Colm smiled down at her through the smoke and din, also appreciating bosom and shoulder. She smiled up at him in the same way she had smiled at the poet, meaning it as much, which was much, enjoying him enjoying her. Warm, intelligent Wanda, non-maniacal nympho. One of the world's, not one of nature's, wallflowers. There was so much inequality in the fates of the sexes. Because she had never married, never fancied those who fancied her (a cruel fate that, for either sex,) she was now never bespoke until the shop was empty. Then she was picked up, last, with the hats and coats, picked up in the hall by some unlucky hunter unable to face the rest of the night alone. Remaindered Wanda.

Dawn appeared, 'Now then, you two –'

'Dawn,' said Colm, 'over there. The one with his hat on. A famous Irish poet and doesn't know a soul. Very shy.'

He didn't look shy, standing away from the wall and muttering, his jowl stuck out.

'Oh,' said Dawn uncertainly. 'Are you sure?'

'Sure I'm sure.'

'Oh, what nonsense! We'll soon shake him out of that!' She rushed off crying 'Begorrah!'; Colm heard a guttural polysyllabled bark and saw Dawn, only momentarily put out, two little red spots in her cheeks, standing her ground.

He watched someone stub out a cigarette dead-centre carefully, on the surface of a rosewood table.

'Let's get some more to drink,' he said, rousing himself; there had been something in the sight which reminded him of much. 'Will you be here when I come back?'

'Yes,' said Wanda simply.

Colm looked round the darkened room and decided that this was probably true, and so, his base as secure as he could make it, he went towards the long table where the drinks were.

The crowd was thickest there, and least yielding. The white tablecloth was soaking now and pulled askew, and from a crate under the table Colm watched someone take a bottle of whisky and make for the hall with it under his coat. After craning over some shoulders, making sure there were some bottles still left, he decided to find the lavatory. Shoving through shouted conversations and under full glasses raised over his head, he pushed a likely door. Edward, Dawn's brother, and Miriam, whose house this was, clothed and cumbrous, were on a bed piled with coats.

Miriam, horizontal, twiddled her fingers in a wave to him and Edward, furious, face blanched with effort and a lock of his careful Etonian hair plastered across his forehead, hissed: 'D'you *mind* !'

'A little,' said Colm, slowly closing the door. Finding the lavatory, he found that he was drunk, which was as it should be, and that the lavatory bowl was called 'The Shark'.

Coming out he found Miriam's husband, intimate on the telephone in the hall; he extended his free left hand for Colm to shake and made pleased-to-see-you-how-are-you faces while he continued his crooned conversation on the phone. His eyes were half-shut and Colm gently pumping his left hand felt dispirited to be the one using his right. He filled two large tumblers to the brim with whisky and carried them back to where he had left Wanda. She was still there. They sat on the floor against the wall, about knee-level to the rest of the party.

'Have you any of those nice cigarettes?'

Colm opened his spare box of fifty and gave her one.

'Keep it dark.'

'What do you know of Dawn's brother?'

'Nothing – except that he's very kindly giving this party.' Colm had an old-fashioned sense of the courtesies and drank some of his host's whisky with satisfaction after saying that.

'I don't understand. Is he a banker or a poet?'

'Both. Just as he is English in America and American here. The most understandable of all human ambitions: the desire to have it both ways,' Colm said, putting out his cigarette in a half-empty glass someone had abandoned by the wall-skirting. The white filter-tip detached itself and sank while the remaining pieces of tobacco floated slowly down like shreds of faecal matter drained from a stomach into a jar.

For some time now he had been watching a girl. She was tall and fair and she didn't move much, stayed where she was and people came to her. Her eyes didn't keep going on and off like other people's. When she really smiled it was with her whole head and with no effort. The men who spoke to her were mostly older ones who looked at her with a special sort of expression on their faces and so did their wives.

Her end of the room seemed a quiet spot, and it looked as if it had become like that because of her. It was characteristic of the hunters that they gave her, the biggest game, a wide berth. This made Colm pleased for them. It showed they still remembered what the game was all about, gave it an honesty it was seldom granted. Was he not himself a hunter?

'Is his book any good?' Wanda was still asking about Edward.

'Of course not.'

'I bet Derek will say it is. Too good a joke for him to miss. He'll enjoy praising it.'

Wanda was no fool. That was true. The one thing Colm could not forgive: a cynicism that Derek imagined was based on a love of the highest. What was the use, Derek would say, of distinguishing between various kinds of mediocrity? – But that left us nowhere, the difference between a man standing up and a man crawling about not worth measuring. How could Derek have been taught the highest at his bloody public school if people hadn't spent two thousand years trying to sort it out for him? You had to believe in a movement towards some sort of Best or you couldn't measure at all. The difference between himself and Derek was not the thickness of a hair but it was all the difference. He believed in perfection – in a world of presences and messages that if only they could be heard and understood, tended, guided towards it – he believed in this possibility of perfection because he had no choice. He felt the presences and heard (muffled as through wads of gauze) the messages. He was hearing them now, oddly, when he looked at the other end of the room, towards that girl. This did not prove they existed. To acknowledge them was a decision merely – a way to live. The education of dreams.

He believed in some sort of life beyond his own because he had found it impossible to think of someone he loved as dead. He acknowledged this and didn't argue with it. It seemed important not to. He talked often to his father, for instance, as though he was away in some distant place. He also spoke to a friend who had killed himself. There were others. These involuntary conversations sometimes made him feel foolish, but he preferred to be his own fool. This irrational faith made his life more difficult, not easier.

He saw Derek detach himself from a group and move towards

the girl he'd been watching. Derek would never share the hesitations of the other hunters.

'Let's dance,' he said to Wanda and stood up quickly. The blood surged painfully to the back of his head and he caught sight of himself in a mirror, his hair sweat-stained, his face red, a bored man who had drunk too much, which is what he was. Wanda stood up obediently and they moved slowly, half-time, to a fast record which was the best Colm felt he could manage and Wanda was a terrible dancer anyway. He sensed a cool breeze coming from the part of the room where that girl was standing as though it was raised a little above ground level. He was going to have to do something about it.

They paused opposite Norman Pinswell, who was confined in a small talking-area by the fireplace with his latest Finn.

'Norman,' said Colm, as they slowed to a halt in front of him.

Norman opened his mouth and made his clicking noise which was surprisingly expressive. Yawing his bottom jaw up and down and clickety-click meant 'Splendid, thank you.'

'Olga – a colleague – Mr Treacey. And –'

Colm introduced Wanda.

Olga looked up, heavy eyed, from a book she had taken from the shelves. 'I never regret what I have lost if I cannot have it back,' she growled in a light bass.

Pinswell looked ahead, pretending to ponder this.

Maybe in her country the students in their student hats swapped these obscurities like stamps. Colm gave it a try.

'Remorse has a thousand fathers but no sons,' he said cheerfully.

Olga turned on him eyes so heavy it was like watching an effort of weight-lifting to see her move them. They were surrounded by thick squiggles of mascara, like relief lines on a map, which gave them a look of goitrousness. Pinswell was staring at him with his mouth open.

'And what do *you* do?' Even the social Wanda sounded at a loss.

'I am a graphic artist.' She stared into Wanda's eyes so fixedly as she said this that Colm was certain Wanda was going to say

How nice out of panic, so he shifted his attention to Simon Pelham, who was standing near.

'How nice,' said Wanda.

What on earth was a graphic artist? A person who drew things? Simon's arm was thrown like a scarf round the squat shoulders of a Central European publisher who always reminded Colm of a deceptively sleepy lizard; at any moment he might flick out a tongue and someone would vanish. He made a good contrast to Simon's open good looks.

It was impossible not to like Simon. He was so unabashed in the enjoyment of himself. For most people the world was a series of dark holes down which they felt required to disappear, like ferrets, either flushing out their prey or emerging, scarred and blinking, with a mouthful of excuses. But Simon strode over the holes and convened everything above ground (or rather The Town, his personality was entirely urban) into an auditorium where its sole requirement was to applaud his performance. This it usually did although sometimes whispering behind its hands. He was wearing a pink cravat fastened by a huge pearl, his collar carefully flowing, his clusters of curls like an etherealized Prinny; he looked magnificent, androgynous and more like a poet than anyone had the right to. The gestures of his free arm were wider than other people's and the publisher, London's leading connoisseur of the smart, was giggling appreciatively. Not the least remarkable thing about Simon (whose innocence it was impossible to doubt) was that he never wasted his charm; those he amused and impressed were always those able to do him some good. It was as though he was perfectly in tune with his time – an interesting but not altogether cheerful thought. Colm had always found it impossible to listen to a word that Simon said.

The wind was still blowing, or rather resting round about him. They were near the girl now, she had her back to him. Even her feet seemed to be calm, and her long legs. She was the only straight line in the room, a pendulum at rest, yet the line of her back was neither confident nor very straight, self-deprecating rather, inquiring.

He heard Olga say 'And *what* was his name?' She was the

only one who resented his straying attention. He remembered that the plainer Pinswell's girls were, the more demands they made, an attempt to outface the world which he approved of.

'Treacey,' he called back.

'A trochee!' groaned Olga. He left Wanda and Pinswell to deal with that.

Still the cool, questioning air. He allowed himself to be held in it, waiting for some cue.

He caught sight of Edward, a shade of grey-yellow as though he had been sick, leaning on Miriam rather than dancing with her, a hand on each of her buttocks, his face drawn with nausea or ecstasy or the effort to stay vertical. Her face, glimpsed over his shoulder, was firm and determined as though she had decided that what she was dancing with might not be much but no one, tonight, was going to take it away from her. Edward suddenly went down on his knees partly dragging her with him and Colm wondered if he was about to revert and howl like a dog. He crawled under the table and was hidden for a moment by the screwed-up table-cloth. He emerged dragging in his teeth the final crate of whisky. Dawn had been speaking to Colm while this was going on, he hadn't heard what she was saying. Following the direction of his eyes she gave one of her shrieks and darted towards the now horizontal Edward. Colm turned and found himself face to face with the girl.

It was like opening a window. The cloud of cool air he had felt round his head for the last half-hour was joined with its source, with hers; they were enclosed for a moment in a different weather. He looked into her big green eyes which had little flecks of brown around the iris as though it had melted, completely preoccupied with a stillness that was happening inside him.

He learned she was Beatrix Pelham, Simon's wife. It didn't seem to matter. He was content to stand there, chains he hadn't known he wore falling away. Then she disappeared, was collected by someone. That didn't seem to matter either. He felt the same when she wasn't there. He felt (he recognized the feeling as though he had always known it would come back – but from where on earth did he remember it?), he felt happy.

'Let's go,' he said to Wanda.

'All right,' she said. They moved towards the hall and Wanda went to get her coat. She returned almost at once as though afraid he might disappear. The hall was near the drinks table.

'Shall we have a quick one?' he said.

'No – but you do,' said Wanda, so he did, as though he had to be drunk to leave with her. It wasn't true, he liked her, but she had sounded so grateful. Why did he have to be reminded of loneliness? Why did he always have to remember jails, diseases, cripples, wars, madhouses, suicides, tortures, murders, corpses *all the time* for Christ's sake! He could live with them; what small order that he could arrange inside his skull would be done in their presence (he still felt that pocket of silence inside him, shrinking a little maybe – he felt an instinct to cup his hands round it) but did he have to take on all of them all at once? Couldn't it be little by little?

They went out into the Earls Court Road to find a taxi and Wanda took his arm.

The night had settled balmy and clear as it often does in London, wasting the good weather after the sun has gone down. The dusty draughts and showers of the day had given way to a warm breezeless still. If the sun had been shining it would have seemed Mediterranean. The ends of parties were spilling out on to balconies over the trees and gramophones sighed through open windows. London, closed in on itself, clenched like a fist, had for once an aspect of openness. People were seen, by shafts of light that fell among the trees, unfurtively together and enjoying themselves. Young men in shirt-sleeves bending over record-players (one accompanied an inaudible record on his own sad trumpet, putting in a soundless pa-poop now and then, his eyes closed), girls in thin, ribbed sweaters, the new breed of girls that seemed to have no flesh under the armpits, their arms were sticks attached to a boyish cylinder upon which, inappropriately, were breasts appliqué like little pointed cakes. How did such wholesale physical changes come about? It was as though there was a reservoir of Girl waiting for a new male fantasy to energize it. Beatrix was not like that. She belonged to a separate, entirely differentiated sex, with its own rules of growth and response; she stood firmly on her long thin feet; she owed no part of her existence to male demand which is why the hunters, apart from Derek, had left her alone.

Colm began to sing as they walked along the Earls Court Road among the groups of tall Australians.

> 'Have you met Sir Jones?
> people said when we first met,
> you were just Sir Jones to me.
> And all at once I caught my breath
> and all at once was scared to death
> and all at once I owned the earth a-nd sky-y.'

he yelled, hearing Ella Fitzgerald's voice, not his own. Commonplace experience – happens all the time. *Commonplace*! Great God! Those few moments were the most awesome thing that had ever happened to him.

Wanda walked at his side, her arm through his. She had seen his face when he was talking to Beatrix. She felt no envy, or very little. She, Wanda, had no claim. She liked Colm for the warmth he gave off always, even at his most absentminded and knew her own limits and his; she dreamed very little.

It was Wanda who noticed the passing taxi, stopped it and gave the driver her own address. This was her world.

Wanda had come originally from a small town in Leicestershire and had found herself a job (something to do with the sale of computers). By diligence, intelligence and her generalized affection for everyone, she had risen to a competence that paid for her clothes and her room and enabled her to seek out a private life unburdened with preconceptions or demands – the female equivalent (a new species still in process of evolution) of the clubbable bachelor man. But, Colm thought, as he settled into his corner of the taxi, she in hers, their hands lying loose on the empty space of the seat between them, there was a taste in her of someone who had decided that there was very little genuinely to celebrate in the world; that she might as well have her share of all the fairly enjoyable, fairly disappointing things. She did not demand enough.

Colm had found this unconscious (or at least unrationalized) disabusement in many girls like her, women now, who had grown up since the war, fairly tough, fairly attractive, irrelevant as a rubber-plant in a pot. He felt for them a huge pity which was the last thing they or anyone else wanted. They left home, found jobs that engaged only a fraction of their attention, involving themselves with men likewise. And with their confounded and superb female adaptability they had put their roots down exactly as far as their soil allowed – no more chafing at the constriction of their pot, the absence of their native atmosphere, than the majority of their Victorian sisters had resented their mysterious husbands and the yearly child.... What was their native atmosphere?

Certainly Wanda's little flat had less of it than the rooms of the most Bedouin of Colm's bachelor acquaintances. It was a place to receive invitations from. On invitationless nights it was somewhere to stop, after rinsing out things in the hand basin, to an early, not very inviting looking bed. It was far more squalid than any male equivalent. There, disorder would have been the relics of a purpose, an uncleaned-up meal, a mess of newspapers, thrown down books, shoes – dirty perhaps, but the personal dirt of lived-in clothes. This was a shell scarcely inhabited at all; a hole for feeling depressed in. He watched her kneel to light the gas fire.

Weren't females meant to be nest-builders? Perhaps both male and female only act out their attributes in the presence of each other? Or perhaps this bare little larder was a comment, again unconscious, on a male dirty trick: women having bravely fought for equal shares, men had handed them the stalest part of the loaf, the lowest reaches of their own impersonal job-and-money servitude. It was true that men pretended their public lives were fun and enviable. They had to pretend; each sex is entitled to its mystery. If women had discovered now just how joyless most of it was, did the fault lie with the men? They had put up with it long enough. As for the upper reaches, as for success, up there, it was every man and woman for himself. Colm, who loved women, almost shrived himself and his sex from any intentional double-cross. If women had thought that competition was all sex and creative ardour, they had bought it. And yet – this flat was awful – far more awful than if it had been a man's. The defeat seemed greater, the loss more important.

Wanda put her arms round his neck, smiling up at him, he had been neglecting her. He responded, summoning enthusiasm, warming to his task.

She broke away. 'I think I'll go and have a shower. Would you like one first?'

'No, thanks.' He had seen through the open door of her tiny bathroom a yellow Victorian geyser he had no desire to tangle with. She smiled as though to say: You nice, dirty men are all the same. 'I am extremely clean,' he felt like answering. He did a quick mental check: well, fairly clean. He'd sweated a lot at the party.

'I'll just have a quick pee before you go in,' he said; she might be ages in there. The lavatory, also Victorian, with a suggestion of flowers round the top of the bowl, was called 'Middlemarch'. She came in before he had finished. Colm knew this was a gesture of intimacy, she was taking liberties with his body because hers was at his disposal, but he wished she hadn't.

In the bathroom mirror, as he turned, he saw her peeling off her false eyelashes. He hadn't noticed she was wearing them. Thank heavens he hadn't swallowed one just now! Turning to him she let her dressing gown fall and stepped into the bath under an antiquated shower arrangement he hadn't noticed. But it was the nakedness of her face that moved him, minus dark eyelashes and make-up, puffy, pale, more exposed than any body could be. She was looking at him, her arms hanging limply by her sides, showing him. Her body, not young, not perhaps ever beautiful, fell away under her quiet gaze in successive folds like the Willendorf Venus. Colm felt a spasm of love confronted by such an entirely simple revelation: these are the goods on offer: we wish they were more.

'I'll leave you to it,' he said. But before he spoke, a fraction before, she had broken the moment and had begun busily soaping herself, flapping her breasts, bending her knees to get between her legs, smiling at him, moment over. But he was grateful she had first done that natural, unsmiling thing, glad he had come, glad that for five seconds she had trusted him and he had been able to respond. He left her to be as hearty as she pleased by herself, and climbed down into the bed. It seemed to be an unfolded couch affair, only a couple of inches above the ground, with a hard line down the middle. Perhaps she unfolded it before going out, just in case.

With his hands behind his head he thought of the day: Findus and his innocent corruption, the appalling Edward, Derek and the roast duck (why did he love Derek so much?): that girl he'd met. He was glad he had not gone home to think about that. He wanted to wear the idea until it fitted him. Where it rubbed he would know to what extent it was badly made. If not, if it became a part of him he would be so changed that without much thinking he'd know what to do. He did not want to spoil a possibility too soon. There was still a pocket inside him, safe for the moment, where there lurked the seeds of an excitement, he could feel them stir.

Wanda appeared in the doorway of the bathroom and reached inside the room, turning off the bedside light. The bathroom light she left on and she stood for a moment darkly framed by it, silhouetted. The moment of truth was over, now was the time for illusion. She paused there, shyly, with a woman's instinctive and inveterate sense of theatre: a female's rather – he'd seen the pigeons doing it on the office window-sill, undeceptively reluctant, arousing the male. Byron was right when he confessed towards the end that on the whole, women were *nicer* than men. They retained this sense of occasion, this need to save things from becoming an undifferentiated blurr. She padded to switch off the gas-fire, walking as though she wore shoes, hard on her heels, her feet flapping on the uncarpeted parts of the floor. Then, still leaving on the bathroom light that gave the small bed-sitting room a glow that made it almost pleasant, she turned and half ran towards the bed, leaping into it and pulling the covers up to her chin, as though now afraid to let him see too much.

Soon he was wrapped in her softnesses and warmths and the hard knots of whisky and fatigue and nicotine in his bloodstream began to dissolve. He found that all day he had been wearing his shoulder-blades a couple of inches too high, as though hunched against some blow; he rediscovered the true length of his neck.

Then Wanda sat up and took something from a little case by her side of the bed, Colm, surprised, couldn't quite see what it was. Then she knelt forward, and, half-kneeling, half-squatting, looking at him all the time, she inserted it inside herself.

'Better be on the safe side,' she said briskly.

Presumably it melted inside her and exuded moistures or gases that killed the seed. Colm was afflicted with one of those *spectra* that came to him frequently, often more vivid than his own surroundings. As clearly as Ben Jonson saw the Tartars and Turks, Romans and Carthaginians fight around his great toe as he lay in bed looking at it, Colm saw white-coated Special Detachments intent on their task, crouching on the roofs of sheds, taking off the small round lids the size of manhole covers, breaking their gas-capsules and dropping them in, closing the holes quickly before the fumes, or the cries of the people inside, could reach them.

He groaned. The clang of those little metal lids! Not here. Not now! Why had she not spared him that! He didn't want her to run any risks for his sake but she hadn't obeyed her instinct, which would have been to hide this; confused by the new concept of sharing – both in this together, no secrets, face up to life! Wanda snuggled again beside him, pretending she had done nothing. Soon he did, more or less, forget.

After a while she slept, her head in the crook of his arm. She looked happy, satisfied with what she had managed to salvage from the day. He was pleased too, lying with her breathing on his cheek, noticing that with the instinctive self-sacrifice of women (which was something he wished they *would* learn to forget) she was sleeping on the hard edge of the divide in the studio couch leaving him the soft bit. He thought of his room which was gathering one more layer of neglect, one degree harder to penetrate, then he too slept.

When he woke it was still early and it was good to find her lying beside him, turned away from him now and slightly snoring. Her little room was the corner of a larger flat the rest of which she rented to a West Indian and an Irish labourer. He had gathered earlier that it would be better for her authority as a landlady if he could manage not to be seen so he decided to leave now, tasting the whisky on his breath, still with the energy of the drink unslept away. She stirred slightly as he dressed and then sat up with a start to look at her alarm clock. It was too early for her to go to work so she went under the clothes again holding out a hand to him and he kissed it and saw her smile and drift back to sleep with a small warm noise.

He opened her door quietly and tiptoed on to the landing. There was the noise of a flushing lavatory and before he could reach the stairs he came face to face with a man, towel round his neck, braces hanging down, his face raw with shaving; an Irish face of the heavy violent sort; long feminine eyelashes, hairy assertive eyebrows too dark for the red colouring and a long argumentative lip. The man stared at Colm and at the door he had just closed behind him, then back again at Colm. Slowly he moved his eyes up Colm and down him, equally slowly closed them, turned his back and walked away. Colm envied his certainty of the importance of what had happened behind that door.

He went out into the wastes of Maida Vale. There was a heavy morning mist and he had no idea where he was. There seemed to be no bus routes. So he turned up his jacket collar against the early chill and began to walk. There were no cafés open yet, but soon there would be and he'd go in and have a cup of coffee; then he'd find a telephone and ring Wanda before she went to work. He would avoid making any further date with her and she would understand. They would bump into each other again, and whether anything more happened would depend on how things were going for them both at that moment. Tonight he wasn't going anywhere, so he'd clean up his flat and do some work. That was the thing! He felt quite cheerful at the thought of this and thrusting his fists deeper into his jacket pockets he began to walk faster. He even began to hum. 'Have you met Sir Jones' and that reminded him of something he had not forgotten. But he wasn't going to puzzle about it. If there was real music there would be no need to invent it. All he had to do was listen.

4

It was Derek, not Colm, who rang me up, which is what I thought might happen.

How can I describe myself in the way I do – this stunning girl Colm met at a party?

There is an excitement in certain meetings that is unlike anything else. That's all I've tried to suggest – how Colm saw me at the time. To help me imagine it I've used what I came to feel myself, how I began to see him.

I want to interrupt this story occasionally because I want to remind anyone reading it that I'm here, a girl, not Colm's dream. Nor is he mine. But a dream-like quality must come in sometimes because that was there as well. What was marvellous was not because it was perfect or because we were. Quite the opposite. It was so in spite of us.

As I say, it was Derek who rang me up first.

He suggested we went to Billingsgate fish-market at six o'clock in the morning to sample some of the pubs that are open there at that time. I couldn't think of any reason to say no, so we went. You had to buy a fish and place it on the bar to show your bona fides before you could buy a drink. The fish passed from hand to hand (there were plenty of people about, not many fish-porters as far as I could see) and after a while I felt sorry for that poor wilting fish. Derek was the sort of man who liked to be in charge, we went only to places where he knew the ropes. I like to share things, surprises and discomforts as well. Men like Derek make me feel protected in the wrong way. However, it is restful. I didn't feel disloyal just tagging along because to Derek it was an elaborate game which he enjoyed. He happened to be playing the wrong one with me, but I knew he would not be hurt when he found out, regard it merely as one of the fortunes of war, a mistaken appreciation of the foe.

A week later he borrowed a two-seater sports car and we went up the Thames Valley past Goring – his idea was that we should find somewhere to swim. It struck me that he was forcing the pace a bit, a swimming twosome with a married woman was a little obvious even for his role as friend-of-us-both. (If I sound cynical I think it will only be to men, who have an affected innocence in these matters, women will know what I am talking about and why I went and quite enjoyed myself.) The skies threatened as we drove and by the time we were near the river it was bucketing down. Derek was nonplussed by this. Then we turned round and drove back. Perhaps I was teasing him, but he was capable of looking after himself. I wanted to see what he would do next.

Another few days passed and he invited me to a poetry reading at the Albert Hall. He had to write a review of it. He warned me it was sure to be awful, but one of the things I had learned about Derek was that he disliked almost everything, which is worrying in a critic. In fact the poetry reading was awful.

A lot of people went to it, mostly young, the queues stretched right round the hall, but once inside, the place is so vast, we formed chilly little groups and no one had the sense to call us down to the front. About half an hour after the scheduled start a bearded man, (massively bearded,) began to make explosive noises and whinnies into a microphone like the impressionist who used to imitate lorries and trains on radio Children's Hour, while three musicians with jazz instruments sat behind him and occasionally blew a note or rattled a drum, as though not sure whether the bearded man was a part of the show. No one took much notice, but when he stopped a few people clapped, so presumably he had been doing something. He looked quite pleased at the applause and kept on bowing even when there was only one person still clapping, high at the back of the hall. In the end the musicians sounded a prolonged farewell note and he was more or less blown off the platform. Then all the lights went out for a long time. You could dimly see figures arguing and gesticulating around the platform. Then the lights came on again and a young man made an announcement which I couldn't hear because he'd forgotten the microphone and then the elderly Irishman who had been at Dawn's party lumbered up the steps and began to read his poems. 'Microphone!' lots of people shouted so another young man rushed up with one and there was much adjusting and scraping to see if it worked and then he started again but you still couldn't hear because he sat too far away and it wasn't turned up enough. This went on for a while and people began to stamp. The Irishman didn't seem to mind, he was wrapped up in what he was reading. When he stopped and went away, who should help him down the stairs but Dawn, she'd clearly become a sort of protectress, shining with responsibility, and I was happy for her. Then I saw Colm.

He was lying almost horizontal, his feet on an empty seat in front of him, an expression of fury on his face. He was alone. Then he got up and spoke to the musicians. They began to play, improvising among themselves. He did something to the microphone. The audience became quiet now. Then various people got on the dais and seemed to be competing with each other who should read next, becoming heated, pulling the microphone from each other until it made growling, fizzing noises. Then the band stopped and watched. Somebody's manuscript was torn in his hand and he stood staring down at it as though his foot had been run over. Colm was back in his place now and looked as though he had gone to sleep. Oddly enough there were microphones (which worked) on the floor of the hall and a couple of young men in the audience had got hold of these and were blowing deafening raspberries into them. Also someone had managed to get to the vast organ at the back of the hall and played blaring similar sounds on that, making everybody laugh. Quite a few of the audience had brought bottles of wine and half-bottles of whisky, were getting pretty drunk and had started necking: other people began to leave noisily even though a rather dotty looking young man in an Eton collar was shouting a poem about undoing bra-straps (I think). Apparently he wasn't a part of the programme because some other (rather sweet-looking) young men pulled him down. His place was taken by a famous poet who lives abroad and has showers of white curls round the face of an educated boxer. He read a couple of poems and that was good, but the raspberry noises continued so he stopped and simply began to chat, which was sad because even I could tell that what he was saying was very silly indeed. It was a disaster all right. Derek was watching the whole thing with an expression like ecstasy on his face. Then Colm saw us.

He came across at once. He said hello to Derek, looking at me, not smiling.

'Let's go!'

'Let's,' said Derek. Colm made a sort of shrugging signal to the band, who looked detached as though the chaos was no concern of theirs. Then he moved his thumb to his mouth, like a spout, as though drinking, and the clarinettist, who seemed to be the leader, gave a little nod, blew a cascade of notes, the drummer banged, the pianist tinkled and then they quickly began to pack up their things. A frantic man rushed to their part of the stand and pleaded, but the clarinettist cupped one hand to his ear as though deafened by the surrounding noise and continued to unscrew the bottom part of his clarinet with one hand, holding the top part between his teeth.

Outside Colm exploded and Derek was amused and calm.

I agreed with Colm. After all, the audience had taken the trouble to come, and had paid.

We went to a pub near the hall and people connected with the reading began to drift in, the musicians first. They were friends of Colm's, he'd laid them on, and they were unruffled. They had known their job if nobody else had known his, so why worry? It was good to see Colm talking to them because he looked happy. I love to watch professionals together; if they respect each other's work so much else goes unsaid and there is a marvellous easiness you don't find anywhere else. We all drank quite a lot and I felt happy myself.

'We just wanted to make contact – you know? – See how things worked out,' one of the boys who had put it on kept saying. He seemed less upset than Colm.

'Yes, but you have to –' Colm stopped himself and then went on more slowly – 'You have to *present* it. Otherwise lights don't go on. Microphones don't work.'

'But we wanted it alive – not a series of crummy turns.'

'So the yobbos take over. What's so pure about that?' He was gentle with them as though almost certain they would not understand. There was an older poet there in a leather jacket who kept snorting behind the younger ones.

'Wish I could have got to read my Vietnam poem,' he said. 'That would have hit those slobs in the guts.'

'No, it wouldn't,' Colm said. 'In the first place they aren't slobs, in the second place they'd never have heard it and in the third place it's a lousy poem.'

'Easy, C.,' called the clarinettist, 'you're talking to the slob we love,' and he laughed, winking at me.

'Oh Christ!' said the poet, 'let me get where I can breathe!' and he shoved past the drummer to the bar, nearly pushing him over. He was a very big drummer but he didn't seem to mind.

'Boy, that one really *cares*!' he said, wiping himself where his drink had splashed.

'What for?' said the clarinettist, 'nookie?' and they all laughed at that. 'Sorry, miss,' he said, tugging a forelock (he was bald), 'that freedom fighter brings out the Common Man in me.' I hadn't known what nookie meant but I guessed.

'The literary life,' I said, not sure what I meant but I liked the clarinettist who was called Bill.

He laughed some more. 'Thank God I'm ignorant!'

Colm was still talking to the two boys. 'Next time – next time –' I thought he was going to warn them against the leather-jacketed poet who exuded the wrong kind of restlessness and was too old for that, but he hesitated and then just said 'Good luck.' They said they wondered if there would be a next time and then they went. The musicians finished their drinks and they too went off after some heartiness among themselves and with Colm. 'Look after him, won't you,' one of them said to me and then 'You're a jammy sod' to Colm.

When they'd all gone the three of us were left alone in the corner and Derek said, 'Why do you bother?'

'With those two kids?'

'With the whole business. It's a farce. Forget it.'

'It's like religion. And Beefeaters. People see a church service carried on by an octogenarian who hasn't had a spiritual insight since Toc H and from that conclude that God is Dead. Those men in flat hats at the Tower of London presenting halberds look pretty funny so the idea of tradition is baloney. Polite people listening to bad poets read bad verses in a religious hush is boring so let's have everybody as impolite as possible. That's real. Start from scratch. Shake the dice all over again.' He groaned and rubbed his eyes with both hands. 'Why must people be such whole-hoggers? It's always either/or.'

Derek nodded over to where the leather-jacketed poet was standing, looking about, but not at us. 'The devil has all the good causes,' he said.

'Doesn't he really care about Vietnam?' I asked. War seems to me always and without exception horrible although when people ask me if I would have liked the Nazis just to take over I get confused and have to shut up. I don't believe I'm wrong, though. What causes wars starts a long way back and so to be asked whether or not you support a particular war is to be asked the wrong question. Instead of blaming war we should be making sure that the things which lead to war are not happening now, which is I think what Colm meant when he said:

'Oh yes he does. Very much. He can get really fond of people he can't see. It's the ones he can see he wants to shoot.'

Derek said, 'Well, there's a lot of bad floating about. Somebody has to do it.'

'Or somebody else will,' chimed in Colm, as though it was a private saying between them, and they smiled.

But I still sensed a worry in Colm and I felt I knew what it was. He thought that what those boys and the poets had attempted was worth a try. He couldn't rejoice that it had gone so wrong. He wondered whether he could have helped, although he never would have involved himself in such a thing, believing it doomed from the start. He refused to believe that poetry and music were condemned for ever to their own small corner singing to themselves. But could they (did they ever) do anything else? It was almost as though I heard these thoughts going through his head and because of what I learned later, I know I was right. With Simon all such worries would have been regarded as pointless because answerless. There is a lot of truth in

Simon's way. But to go on plucking at difficult questions is a kind of truth also and one I found that I longed for.

I felt Colm giving off a glow of life, warm as a radiator. Not decisiveness, activity, which often looks like life and sometimes is, but more often is a sort of self-deafening. It was as if the whole surface of him was exposed to his own questions. Perhaps he would never answer any – he would always be a difficult man, perhaps not even a very special one – he was neither a god nor a fool. But he was alive. I had never felt so at home with anyone.

It was an odd feeling, miles from the crushes I had known as a girl. We sat at the small pub table, Colm on my left, Derek on my right, and there was no question of choosing between them. I was with Colm and he had hardly spoken a word to me.

Derek was marvellous. Without a word or a sign he had given me up. I wasn't sure whether Colm knew this, but Derek did and so did I. His play for me, how seriously he'd meant it I don't know, hadn't worked and so, like a man totting up the risks on a bet, he'd decided not to go on.

'Look, Beatrix, I'm sorry about this, but I'd really better get back and try to describe this evening's *festa*. Can I drop you home?'

'Yes, we'd better –'

'Unless you're eating out, Colm? I don't want to break things up, but I must go really.'

'What? Oh. Can't you stay for a bit?' He turned to me.

'A bit.'

'Good. Are you sure, Derek?'

Derek was quite sure and sorry, etc., and couldn't resist adding proprietorially before he went, to me, 'I'll ring you.'

Colm and I alone for the first time, and for the first time embarrassed. I could hardly blame Derek for leaving behind that small piece of irritating grit. I reckoned it was up to Colm to make the transition and he tried.

'Would you like another drink?'

I said I would although it wasn't true; but I knew he needed time to get used to being unexpectedly stuck with me. I needed time too, for I saw the kind of danger I was running, quite different from anything before. I was a little afraid, but how could

I tell whether it was a prudent fear or just the ordinary kind? I refused to get bogged down at this stage and so I simply watched Colm buying the drinks.

I wasn't at all surprised to be with him. Even his clothes seemed familiar: a thin, light-coloured raincoat and a blue woollen shirt. He looked serious at the bar, and self-contained, not fidgeting. When he turned to the barmaid there was a fold of flesh along his jawline, the kind that on a woman looks like a double chin but on a man looks good. But also, though not in a troublesome way, as though he would always be in control of it, he looked vulnerable. Then he turned right round and smiled at me, catching a smile that I hadn't known was on my face.

He brought over the drinks and sat down and we began to talk – about Dawn's party I think it was; just chat. I don't know what I expected. Then he looked at my drink.

'You don't want that, do you?'

I was going to have to watch my step. Simon would never have noticed that.

'Shall we go?' He gulped down his beer. 'Do you mind if we don't go anywhere very grand? I haven't much money on me.' He looked at me quickly.

I thought: He knows I've got more money than he has. But what a question! ... My heart sank. Nobody's quite sane on the subject of money or sex, and when they're muddled up together it's bad. If you accept the advantages of an inheritance you have to put up with the strains it causes. The only thing you're not allowed to feel is that money doesn't matter because that's too easy. But what did Colm expect me to say? 'In that case I'll go home?'

We went somewhere quite near the pub. Although I could take you there, show you the table where we sat, it's not really a visual memory I have of the next couple of hours. What I felt was the shape of the room enclosing us, our relations in space to each other, our relations in time too, because it was as if those measured walls contained a measured piece of time which was, for us, a pause granted for recognition. The sense of being on a moving belt, always moving on and past, disappeared. We saw and heard each other properly and all the other sights and sounds were not distractions but helpful. It was an extra degree of attention granted, it really seemed, from outside – it was so unexpected. The kind of attention we should give to the whole of life maybe but we go boss-eyed if we try. Here there was no effort. It was natural, as if all the other, inattentive, times were the aberration.

Colm talked, drank a lot of wine which we brought with us from the pub and chain-smoked cigarettes from a large box, while the waitress criss-crossed behind him.

He told me he was a musician, which I had gathered. He had hardly any small talk when he was drinking, but threw out statements and questions that in anyone else would have been overblown but with him were short-cuts, showing you who he was, finding out about you. It was an edited version of himself he gave, staging what he said, with a gesture of his face or hands, ruffling his hair and grinning, or pursing the fingers of one hand together and putting them on his forehead, glancing up at you as he did so, partly apologetic, partly comic. He invited you in but stood aside as he did so, watching. If he started talking about something along a line that didn't mean much to me, he knew at once and switched to another angle. Sometimes I felt I could conduct his conversation with my thoughts. I've never known anyone so responsive or who wasted so little time – we entered each other's lives without ever a direct question. Also I'd never met a man before (except Simon) who didn't have a special kind of talk for women. Perhaps he was not afraid of them. He talked about what interested him, and if you talked he listened. Underneath all the talk was the extraordinary ease we were both feeling.

I must have said something obvious about the musician thing because he said:

'Yes, but why? O.K. Sometimes, rarely, a musician *hears* something he sees. A crowd in a street, say, a bus passes, pigeons fly up, the street has a certain curve to it. These chime together and he hurries home to write it down. If he's lucky a few puzzled people play it to a few more puzzled people. If he's very lucky he gets a commission so he can wander about waiting for more things to chime. Or he can sit on his bum and try to *make* them chime. Why? I'm not talking about the Plight of the Artist, God help us, but is that a way to spend a life?'

He laughed and looked at me and filled our glasses.

'Why not?' he said. 'I think.' He was like a catherine wheel, he spun but the middle stayed dark.

'That thing tonight – those verse writers. (Poet's a big word – a caste-name. Only other people can call them that when they're dead.) All they wanted to do was come out of their rooms, join and be joined. So did the poor bleeders who paid to hear them. It needn't have been such a shambles, but would it ever have worked? Yet the idea's natural enough. As it is everyone goes off on his tod, unjoined, unjoining. Maybe it's this city, too big for the people in it.' He chomped on his food for a bit. 'But why blame it on anything. It is. Always was.'

'Derek didn't seem very concerned.'

'He *was* concerned – years ago. You are looking at the ashes of Derek's old concerns. Out of any hard bits of clinker left he's built himself a little cinder house and inside it he tries to drag any cinder pleasures that will fit. Very sensible. His Scottish mother would have said he cuts his cinder coat to suit his cinder cloth. Perhaps we should all do that. Why go belly-aching after abstracts that have already caused enough trouble?'

'But what about these chimes? I think I hear them sometimes.'

'I'm sure you do. Derek says they're liver.'

'They're what?'

'Digestion. Despair – bad digestion. Joy – good digestion. Look at the way the saints fasted. Mystical experience – non-digestion.'

'You're fond of Derek.'

'Admire him enormously. What courage! No half-baked mysteries. No Perhaps-God, Prime Mover, Holy Humanism, Personal Relationships, Only Connect-edness, for him. He manages without. These chimes – all this going off like a Tonibell Icecream van – perhaps we're just terrified of silence. Derek gives it the two fingers and tries to fill it up with what he finds around him. He isn't forever pulling at things beyond his reach. He isn't scared.' He grinned. 'Makes what he writes damned dull.'

'You don't seem very scared.'

'I'm not, at this moment.... It doesn't do just to be cheery though, does it?'

'Doesn't it?'

'You have to say hello to the black hole underneath first.'

That startled me, because of what I'd seen, that night with Simon.

'You really have to look into it. Then, lightness, dancing on top – that's the best thing there is. Who knows? If you get light enough you might not fall in. You might even take off.'

'What about others?'

'Caring for them, whether they fall in or not?'

I nodded. Thinking about less fortunate people makes you very serious unless you're a great saint. Colm busied himself lighting a cigarette and looked at the floor.

'It's just possible,' he said, still looking away, 'just possible – that we can worry about them too much ... or rather, there are other things to think about first. Which is I think the last heresy there is left to commit,' he added cheerfully. 'I've succeeded in shocking myself.'

'We're all waiting for the stranger. Some enchanted evening, across a crowded room,' he said, looking at me again. 'Forsooth!'

'And you?'

'Of course.'

'It needn't be as stupidly cosy as that.'

He said nothing, looking at me over his cigarette, his eyes narrowed to avoid the smoke.

'Is Derek waiting?'

'Oh, Derek's quite different. He's a quantity man. Uses up what little time has been granted him by an indifferent Fate. Shouldn't be surprised if he kept a score. Not to gloat over. To make sure he's working hard enough.'

'You mean he's never been in love?'

'That's not a kind of Merit Test we have to pass. If anything surprising of that kind has happened to Derek I'm sure he put it down to Dame Kind. Mother Nature taking the fading organism by the scruff and forcing it to reproduce itself.'

'Oh! Such *silliness*!'

'You're very beautiful.' He said it so well I blushed. 'You make me believe beautiful things are possible.' There wasn't much I could say to that or wanted to. His face looked as though he meant it.

'And Simon?' he said.

I was feeling so good I didn't hear at first. Then I did.

What did he think he was doing? I loved Simon. If the time ever came to ask such a thing the question was *mine* not his! Was there something destructive about him? The ability to see and then the desire to spit? There was something hateful in his face now. No, that's not quite true – hateful compared to the simplicity before. Now he was grinning like a man who knows he's made a mistake and is prepared to bluster it out.

The rest of the meal became like any other except for the sick feeling I had. He was attentive and funny in a way he obviously knew how to be and so do plenty of others. Perhaps it had all been a false start. If it was, after that certainty I'd been in, then there was really nothing to trust, only the dark hole, certainly not myself. Yet the anger I felt was a new kind.

Just as we stood up to leave he said, 'Do you have difficulty making up your mind?'

'Sometimes.'

'You know what Derek does?'

'You talk a lot about Derek.'

'He's my anti-self. I believe in lots of things you can't talk about without getting lost in a vast woolly vest. Derek doesn't, but he manages to keep warm without, warmer than I do. I use him as a sort of gauge. Where we part company I know here my believing bit begins. After that it gets very woolly indeed – perhaps sinks into the Ultimate Chilprufe . . .' He looked doubtful.

'Believe what sort of things?'

It was an odd subject to start on, standing between the tables waiting for our change.

'D'you want that wine?' He finished off my glass and we went out to find a taxi.

'What does Derek do?'

'What? Oh, yes. When he's in doubt he puts the reasons For in one column and the reasons Against in another.'

'And adds them up?'

'I suppose so.'

'You seem to take him very seriously.'

'Derek? He's a hoot. The rational principle pushed, rationally, to madness. I love him like a brother.'

In the back of taxis the seat is so wide that for each to sit in separate corners seems unfriendly, to make any move towards each other too artificial, unless it just happens. There are men (not only young ones) who plunge across the intervening gap like footballers diving for the line, as though there was a taxi commandment 'Thou shalt pounce' or, more negatively (like most commandments), 'Thou shalt not not pounce.' Colm was not one of these. But we were conscious of the space between us. The thread that had seemed to join us was broken but the bits were still there, waiting to be put together. Or, no, it hadn't broken, it had gone slack, Colm had stretched it too far.

'I'd like to see you again,' he said at last, business-like. So I knew we would meet again, had known it all along I think. It was because of this sureness that I said, 'What about Simon?'

'I'm sorry I said that! I had reasons. I dare say they weren't good ones ...' His voice trailed away and he looked out of the window. Then he turned. 'But I would like to see you again.'

'All right.'

'How?'

'That's up to you.' (I'd withstood a few of Colm's obliquities, he could surely work out a few female ones in his turn. It was small and silly, I enjoyed it and he jumped like a cracker.)

'Christ, I know that – but *how*?'

'Telephone?'

He looked gloomy. I'd already learned he detested the telephone. He was thinking he might get Simon. I was sure we would meet, the rest was up to him.

Just then the taxi stopped outside where I lived. I put my hand on the door-handle, reasonably slowly – I didn't want to look as though I was bursting to escape, although, a little, I was. A lot had happened this evening – to me at any rate; I wanted to think about it by myself for a bit. The small game of sexual shuttlecock we seemed to have begun was not good enough after what had gone before. Self-consciously 'decisive' men can be restful, they act while you think. Colm left me with at least half the responsibility. That was tiring until one had decided, oneself, what one really wanted. His kind of wholehearted attention to what the other person was thinking and feeling was very demanding; a blessing, but a mixed one.

I turned to look at him to say good-bye and his face had gone simple, he was really looking at me again. All the muddy waters that washed over him (there was nothing 'perfect' about Colm) were gone, and out of them he had retrieved the self that could distinguish what was important and know what to do. I saw he would always have the strength to do that, to pull out of himself the best things when they were needed. The air in the taxi was alive again, we were both alive again; he had done it by a brute effort. I don't think there is anything more difficult than that, the rescue of slipping things before they fall away into emptiness and clatter. There's no leverage, you have to do it from yourself.

Then he kissed me, which would have been silly seconds before and was right now. It was not a passionate kiss – he didn't push us further than the point we were. He kept hold of my hand and really just touched my lips with his and kept them there and I didn't move. I smelt his smell (compounded of cigarettes and wine and his own smell) and felt the firmness of his face on mine and I really had a kind of glory, an immense gratefulness that he had managed to save us both, save the moment, had been able at last to do the simple thing and exactly right. Oh, that is rare! And the rightness was a guarantee of the rightness of what had gone before – truth breeds truth if we only don't get in the way. He had got out of the way, for both of us, just in time. There were dangers, terrors, but what I felt was just this glory.

I got out of the taxi (I'd never taken my hand off the door-handle I realized) and climbed the steps to the front door. As I searched for my key in my bag I saw Colm watching me, still that expression of complete attention on his face, sitting forward on the seat. He hadn't spoken at all. We looked at each other, he turned away and then all I saw was his sharp profile talking to the driver. They drove off; I don't think he turned back (difficult to tell through the smoked blue glass of the back window) and I let myself into the house.

My first impression in the hall was that everything was dusty-looking, as though the colours had faded. I remembered that feeling from childhood – coming back from a party, or after Christmas, ordinary unenhanced reality sombre and lifeless and one was inclined to sulk.

But childhood over-excitement could spoil things, end in tears at just the wrong time. There was a record already on the gramophone. I switched it on and poured myself a glass of whisky.

I don't often do that. I don't really like whisky.

Simon was away working on a television film about East End pubs. He would not be back until tomorrow.

But peaks do exist – and if you're lucky enough to be plumped on top of one (climbing seems to have nothing to do with it) the least you can do is look around and enjoy it and try to understand what you see.

As I said in the beginning this house and these things have never really become my shell – they are Simon's and we share them. But this is my home and I am Simon's wife and anything that had happened or would happen had to include this. Sitting there with my whisky and the gramophone churning there was horror at the thought of compartmentalizing my life – Colm in one box, Simon in another – me flitting between both. Horror of sentimentalizing it, turning it soft for myself.

'And Simon?' ... If he was here now would I tell him? What? That I'd met a super bloke I rather fancied going to bed with? (False toughness is so silly, leaves out too much.) I wouldn't say that because it wasn't how we talked to each other or how either of us thought. *What* then? That Colm had made me feel a warmth and a possibility that he, Simon, had never made me feel? No one could say such a thing. Perhaps the same had happened to Simon, or would in the future? He would not tell me and he would be right. There is nothing, because there is too much, to tell.

I felt a great sadness, the first, I really think, with Simon. I was willing to deceive him about how I felt and what I did when he wasn't there, for the first time, and there seemed no choice. And what about Sam and Cleo, the children? ... No, that was too early, too melodramatic.

Then I began to laugh because I was doing more or less what Colm said Derek did, working out the pros and cons and weighing them up. I saw Derek sitting at home filling out his two columns: For – She has a good figure. Against – She talks a lot. He might as well blow on dandelions. So might I.

But what would happen between Simon and me – and to all this I was sitting among, this record of my late girlhood, our growing up together? It would change, this small attempt at permanence, nothing would ever be the same now. Even Simon would *mind* that – and I loved Simon. Deception, adultery, lies ... no – sticking other people's labels on things is only another kind of self-indulgence. There was a joy inside me as real as my arm and the arm of the chair I sat in and it made its own demand, kicked like a baby inside me, trying to live. To suffocate it because it was 'wicked' (inconvenient?) would be far more wicked.

I wasn't just a restless young woman planning an adventure. There is a kind of self-pity in self-contempt like that. If we cannot trust our brief moments of certainty, what can we trust? Nor did I feel that my new concern was too small, too personal, irrelevant to the larger world outside. Far from it. Although it's true you can be too content to huddle inside your private life, closing your eyes to the rest, I felt this was as large as I could hold, and only by allowing it fully to hold me would I ever be large enough to see the world as it really was; even, in however small a way, be of some use in it. This is what I had been looking for; it was my beginning.

Then I heard what was playing on the gramophone. The record had come to a bit where three people were singing together, very soft and waily, a man and two women. It was Così fan tutte and it was the song they sing when the two men pretend to go off to the wars, the girls appeal to the winds to blow gently for the men as they sail away. The man who sings with them knows that his friends are not really going away, that they're playing a trick to test the faithfulness of the girls. They come back disguised and the girls fall for them, only the wrong way round. The whole thing could be cynical, a send-up of romantic love (Beethoven found it shocking). It is partly a send-up but also it's nothing of the kind. This beautiful song to the wind, founded on illusion, is nevertheless still *beautiful*. The girls are unfaithful, the men play them a silly trick, but the song of love they sing is full of love. They believe it, so it is there. It is as though the love is what matters, not the object of love. Also there is a kind of distant laughter in it, and that is best of all.

I am trying to describe the sudden freedom that I felt as I listened to the lovely wailing noises those three people (and Mozart) were making. So foolish, so soon to be false. A convenient freedom you might say. Yes, convenient, and at that moment complete as though a new kind of oil was round my bones. Love cannot exist without an object, and I love Colm. I admitted that. But whatever happened, to me, to Colm, to Simon, Sam, Cleo, to anyone else who was involved, it was the love that was important. This was such a huge truth (I saw) that it might indeed lose its vividness and shrink back into an excuse for doing what I wanted. But that isn't what I saw at that moment. 'Love God and do as you like' – I understood for a moment what a terrible command that was. Details, events, duties, confusions would intervene so that I'd lose sight of that colossal freedom in which henceforward I was bound to believe. A freedom with an unerring sense of its own goal. I'd lose sight of the goal maybe. I don't think many people can embark on something for long without getting muddled. I can't. But here, now, inside me was this huge warmth that was bigger than I was, bigger than – 'bigger than both of us', that old Hollywood joke.

As I thought of that, the joke we all laughed at in the old films, I remembered that it was funny because it always had been an excuse for doing something fatuously sentimental. I closed my eyes (to try and keep the sureness in, I suppose, like closing the door to keep in the warmth). Then I put on that song again, moved back the needle, and there it still was, that sureness. So I let it surge inside me until it seemed to expand inside my ribs and move up into the corners of my shoulders, completely take me over, spread down my legs and into my feet and toes, up into my cheeks, my eyes, into every cranny in my head, it was an anchored floating, I was more free than I'd ever been because I'd found a place. I was in love, and was I to be ashamed of it? It was like swimming alone in the sea when the sun is shining and the water is warm. All you can see in front of you is the low curve of the horizon and you give yourself to the water, let it wash over you and bear you up: infinite, yielding, and strong. There is danger in it too. But for the moment the greater danger, because it is a kind of crime, is to turn too soon and splash back, safe and unaffected.

5

Charles Findus woke up and sighed; as he usually did when he woke up. In his sleep he seemed to inhabit an altogether larger and easier ambience. He was very fortunate in his night-life he considered. It was always something to look forward to: close his eyes, wait for not long and there he was; difficult to say where exactly, but a universe infinitely better tailored to his tastes. However each morning, on waking, he gathered his forces and chid himself; he did not believe in dreams.

His watch said eight o'clock, held close to his eyes, his spectacles were strategically placed on the dressing-table so that he had to commit himself to being out of bed if he wanted to see properly – the princely galleries he stalked through all night were difficult to relinquish. So with his left hand he turned back a triangle of bedclothes at the same time landing his feet squarely on the floor. He set some store by the rhythm of this unflinching beginning to the day. The clean outlines were blurred, as usual, by the usual fumble for the glasses (still sitting on the bed, it was a very small bedroom he was in these days) but soon these were adjusted over his ears, their earpieces of thin elasticated metal with little knobs on the end snapping pleasantly into place. He was awake, he could see and (he could feel) it was a warm morning. He lingered, looking at his feet. Not bad feet, somewhat gnarled perhaps but not at all veiny – however, they were not a young man's feet. When did one begin to *feel* old? He had always imagined an appropriate change took place in the mind as the body changed. He unhitched his pyjama jacket, pulled the fastening of his trousers like a ripcord and let them fall. He looked down. Had his body changed all that much? There were things it no longer *wanted* to do, certainly, but where were the unmistakable portents of the decay that had undoubtedly taken, and was taking, place? Visible to others perhaps. Not to him. Death was a long way off. And death, until it came rattling loud and clear, was not to be thought of. He believed, because he chose to believe, in the Future, the ultimate social perfectibility of Man. Yes. There were things one chose to believe just as there was food one chose to eat. The best thoughts were the ones that made you function best. He, Charles Augustus Findus, functioned not badly, not too badly at all.

He went downstairs in his dressing-gown to put on the kettle, upstairs again to wash and shave. Kettle boiled, he made their morning tea and dressed and shaved and shining, he took a cup to Margaret. Since her illness she had slept on the ground floor to save climbing the stairs, and Charles had exiled himself to the spare room; he had not enjoyed sleeping in their bed without her.

She stirred, she had taken a sleeping pill, and then smiled up at him sleepily from her sofa-bed in the sitting-room. She wore her bright-brown hair in short plaits at night and it made an old-fashioned frame for her face lying on the pillow, reminding him of his mother and of himself as a small boy.

'Shall I open the curtains? It's rather a nice morning.'

'Do – but not too wide,' she murmured, not sitting up. Margaret had always been a very slow waker.

He went quickly to the window, feeling rather spring-heeled, and carefully drew the part of the curtain that would not let the morning sun reach her. It fell instead on his own face and then on to the rug in a flat beam full of motes, low-angled spring sunshine that made the rug look faded and the room more like a sick-room than it should. However, he knew the sun would soon be blocked by the house opposite and the room would return to its usual, supportable glow. Do the well despise the sick? Why else did he now, in this room, feel so well, almost spry in fact? He had to quench a desire to whistle.

When he was about ten years old he had seen a weasel kill a rabbit. At first he had thought the rabbit was leaping for joy; it was a cold bright morning in January. Then he heard it scream and noticed round its neck a tiny circle of brown, not much thicker than a grown-up's finger. Then the big rabbit gave a last turning leap almost in front of him and fell on its back, still kicking. The brown necklet detached itself and became a thin streak of purpose that ripped and tore at the rabbit with a head like a needle, pulling out strings of insides that smoked in the cold air, hurrying off with them, running back for more, the rabbit still alive. Charles had been about to call his mother to look at the funny rabbit and it was all so quick that the call was still in his throat when the weasel disappeared, leaving behind a still, steaming, mess of fur and bones. He never told her, or anyone. Somebody at school had called him a rabbit, because of his short-sighted habit of wrinkling his nose to push up his spectacles. He decided he was not going to be one. Or a weasel either; horrible; he had no desire to win; but no weasel was going to get him either. No weasel had – so far. Absent-mindedly he touched the wood of the mantelpiece. A negative achievement perhaps, but so it was.

Was there, however, an element of weasel-rabbit in his unusual heartiness in the presence of the sick Margaret?

'You're very cheerful this morning?' she said, looking at him standing in the sun.

Resentment? Is the relation of the sick and the strong always, in some degree, one of mutual displeasure? These were ideas that occurred to Charles as he imagined they must to every man, but he knew how to deal with them. He ignored them. They bore no relation to himself and Margaret (the possible death of whom was something he also ignored), so why break his head on them? There were times, he had to admit, when he had a sense of his head as an overstuffed cupboard bursting with shoved-away unanswered questions. A condition of life, he presumed. And if the cupboard should become too crowded, the door burst open. ... Sufficient unto the day. He put his resilience down to fortunate health.

But there was another, worse thing. By not thinking of such matters, Margaret's death for example, and what he could possibly do without her, was he stocking up for himself shocks and outrages he would be unprepared for if they came? That hatred of cruelty for predators, was perhaps not enough to get one man through life. Had he reached the age of fifty-two safely, reasonably happily, only by leaving too much out?

He went to sit beside Margaret. She had been looking at him all the time, her head still on the pillow. She should have married someone else, he thought, someone altogether livelier, funnier, *nobler*. His life was all very well for him, but she had been designed for brighter things.

'I don't like you being ill.'

Margaret laughed, 'I should think not!', levering herself up in the bed, Charles helping her with the pillows; she took her tea from him. 'You're funny to watch in the mornings. You go about debating with yourself. Sometimes it looks as if the opposition is winning. Then you find a formula and everything's all right again. It does me good to see you.'

'Pleased with myself?'

'Not as pleased as I would like you to be. Most of us are too *dis*pleased with ourselves. Maybe we have reason.' She smiled.

'Haven't I?'

'Yes,' said Margaret, and began to chuckle. 'I like to watch you, that's all.' She drank her tea. 'I've been thinking of Malcolm.' (Their son who had died.) 'Odd there are so many things lying about in one's mind one can't quite get hold of. It's as though there's something I want to remember, but whenever I try it just moves a little bit further out of reach. You know the way you dangle a ribbon for a cat? Teasing, jerking it away? It's just like that sometimes – as though one's mind is playing a game. Although of course if you tease a cat for too long it suddenly pretends the ribbon isn't there and carries on washing itself.'

At the mention of Malcolm the cupboard door inside Charles's head began to rattle and bang. He got up and went to the window again.

'Charles.' She called him back firmly. 'Cat with nine lives!' So she *had* thought of him as the cat, washing himself, ignoring the ribbon. But her voice was so warm it couldn't hurt him. 'Charles – I'm loopy in the mornings after these pills and tired when you get home at night. It's horrid. There's something you ought to know about my kind of illness; it's not nearly as bad *inside* as it looks to you from the outside. It makes one so marvellously important to oneself. So think of us as fully occupied please, my illness and I. Anyway, I intend to get better. What about the holiday?'

'Do you think you'll be able to make it?'

'Of course! You don't think I've retired to my rugs and vapours forever do you? I'm wrapping myself in all this like a cocoon. I'm more than three-quarters enjoying it, and you know it. I thought you'd started to fix everything?'

'I do have a scheme in hand. There's a chance I may move a step up the hierarchy.'

'Charles – how marvellous!'

They both had roughly the same attitude to his job. Her pride in him was a game they both enjoyed.

'When shall we go?'

'Well – it hasn't happened yet –'

'Can't we go anyway?'

'Of course we can. But this promotion would give the Puritan in me an excuse. Reason for celebration. Also, it would be nice not to have to pinch. I thought about the middle of next month?'

'The South of France in May! Oh, Charles!'

She was like a girl. She is a girl, thought Charles. And I'm a bald pot-bellied boy. What *is* growing old?

'Now go and eat your beastly bran – you'll miss your train.'

Charles went to the kitchen to fix himself a bowl of dried nuts and raisins and other, unidentifiable, things, a Swiss preparation that carried him unrumbling through the morning. He had stopped Margaret getting breakfast – she took nothing herself – and quite enjoyed this stuff. Spooning it into his mouth, standing in the kitchen, he began as usual to look forward to his day. This he regarded as the second greatest of his strokes of good fortune: that he enjoyed the hole he had found for himself, it suited him. The foremost good stroke was Margaret.

But he was glad to be leaving her, knowing he would return. Enjoyed the feel of his official self settling round his shoulders as he strode past the pub to the station. They'd taken down the umbrellas, presumably these were unfurled like flags during licensing hours. The tables looked as nasty as ever in the sullen light, the sun having exhausted itself with that twenty minutes of early-morning shine. There were figures who nodded to him on the platform as he bought his *Times*. There was room in the train, it still only filled up at the next station. He settled himself happily into a corner and opened his paper at the sports page.

And Margaret was pleased to see him go. She had spoken the truth about her cocoon. She found it hard to imagine any life that allowed other lives, nowadays, to impinge on it less. This had always been her ambition (she thought, without remorse), to become her own shape, allowing no one and nothing to unshape her. Exactly what it was, her shape, she had not yet discovered – that was her preoccupation – and she welcomed the chance to settle back into herself, tasting, allowing the thoughts and memories to group and regroup, assert themselves or fade. She considered herself blessed to have leisure to do this and asked nothing more of life.

She thought often of Malcolm: or rather she allowed the memory of him as a baby, a young child (it was chiefly her helpless, surprised emotion for him that she remembered), lead naturally and astonishingly to the moustached young man, defiant, more than a little shifty, haunter of roadhouses and second-hand car dealers that he had become, and then his death and the physical snap she had felt inside her, as though they had still been connected, this noisy stranger, infrequent visitor, and herself. How little she had felt besides! Or rather how much, but for a life that seemed to her meaningless, unbearably devoid of shape or point, perhaps not really for Malcolm at all. Her fault? Very possibly.

Was it dreadful to ask so little of her own life – only seeking to be, conscious of that being, savouring it? She couldn't feel guilt. That she felt when she bestirred herself in a way that was false for her. She had come across a sentence by Coleridge: 'There is something inherently mean in Action.' That had made her laugh out loud. Yes, she had felt that often!

Was there, she wanted to find out, a Substance called 'Margaret'? Or was she just a hook upon which Accidents were hung? Surely she was more than the sum of the things that happened to her? By reducing those things to a minimum she hoped to discover what.

Malcolm had been a mystery to Charles as well. Just as she was. But that was a mystery she made sure continued. Not to any tormenting extent, but there was in Charles a turning away from mystery, a too facile determination to put everything squarely in the light of day (as though daylight did not contain as many shadowy deceptions as the dark!) and the mystery he seemed to find in her kept him in touch (perhaps) with that large area into which she lowered herself like a bucket. Really – it was an orgy of self-love, her life! Even the small duties she performed for Charles, keeping his house, keeping him happy, these were only pleasures. Everything she did pleased her, it was disgraceful! But in the early days, forcing herself to feel guilt at her easy content, when she had made herself active in any ordinary sense, it had always seemed less than sense to her. She had taken in typing at one stage. Pounded through manuscripts at so much an hour. Even if (as happened not more than twice or three times) the manuscript was not dreary, had been worth writing in the first place, what a weight of self-hood it nevertheless seemed to contain! Admirable perhaps, a source of energy, but to her disturbing, irrelevant. Conscious of her luckiness, conscious always of the pain of the world, she had tried directly to do Good Works. Had joined a Meals-on-Wheels service and taken hot food to old people too infirm to leave their rooms or look after themselves. The dirt and ill-temper she had met there, and the generalized kindliness she had been forced to show, had not surprised or frightened her, she had imagined no less. But somehow she had known that for her all this was a charade. There was a waiting-list of willing Meals-on-Wheelers. Her defection would hurt no one; and because for her the situation of these old people, and her own, formed part of a mystery too great for these stop-gaps, she decided to give it up. She might well need a Meal-on-Wheels herself one day, she did not fear that, nor was it the point. The organization had been sorry to lose her. She was pleased when told that some of the old people had asked for her specially, 'the kind lady'. The *kind* lady! Anything she had been able to bring them over and above their meal, if anything at all, had come she knew from these periods of silence into which she so eagerly withdrew. She had left.

Of direct 'charity' she still did a certain amount. From what Charles gave to keep the house (he spent very little on himself) she saved as much as she could, he never noticed. Some she gave away to any of the world charities that advertised in the papers, complete with unthinkable, barely assimilable photographs. (What was the civilization that had to be spurred into awareness by such overt assaults on its complacence!) The rest she kept for him should she die first. In spite of his feeling about inherited money he could hardly refuse a bequest from her of his own saved earnings. Two afternoons a week she read to a blind friend who lived not far away.... How petty it all was, totting up her good deeds like this! Really, she felt not the smallest need to justify herself; she was only checking yet again, feeling so happy, whether there was anything else she could immediately do. The great world outside, greatly suffering, called on her to participate. Money, soup-kitchens – necessary, alas – did not fill the bill, not for her. Millions starving on the plains of India, wars, families wandering homeless even in her own country, to bustle and aid was good. But she felt them calling her in a different way, one she hesitated to put into words. She seemed asked to go down, like a pot-holer, into the dark of herself, a vast cave the size of the world, and to search until she found the small flame of a humanity she shared with all those suffering others. She wanted to squat, naked and humble, by that flame in the dark, among all the other tiny flames, thousands of millions of them, their combined light no greater than the light of one, quite unable to illuminate, even to show the approximate size of, the vast cave in which all equally but individually shone. That would be to taste the fact of being alive to the full!

She stirred, aware of the dangers of the comfort in which she allowed herself these thoughts. She got up, put on a long cotton dressing-gown with a pattern of large softly-coloured flowers on it and gingerly drew open the rest of the curtains, ashamed to find herself blinking in the diffused, yellow-grey light. Then she sat on the bed, undid her plaits, and began swiftly to brush her hair. without a mirror, that was upstairs and she was determined to mend herself, to take no risks at all for the next few weeks. She enjoyed her incapacity a great leal less than she had pretended to Charles, and she regretted the mirror. Her small handbag one could not tell her whether her face was yet too old for such long, young hair. Women whose hair has outlasted their skin tended to overdo it, show it off, and the young-textured hair made their faces look older, the discrepancy even witch-like. But Charles liked it long. All men were sentimentalists about hair.

He still believed she should have married someone more dashing: a great poet – a goodness knows what! Let him, it did him good. She smiled to think of it. As if she had ever sought that kind of intensity! Well – perhaps once or twice when she was a young girl she had felt a desire to burn, to let all the heat inside her rise to the surface in one great apotheosis of flame ... her self becoming a black flake, a feather of ash on the wind, crumbling back into air. She laughed as she continued brushing. She was much too substantial for that! She had never fancied the partial conflagration, the sort that leaves behind it a mess of dark, sticky grit. Had she been too frightened perhaps? Oh, the fear of fear! How we force ourselves! Charles was exactly the right size for her if only he knew it. (Why should she tell him?) What was missing between them – if there *was* anything – it was perhaps exactly that which set her free. The happiness she had found was the one that fitted her. Let others have opinions about whether it was adequate or not. How could they possibly know?

It was true she dreamed more than he did, day-dreamed. The habit had settled on her when she was a child in Scotland. There had been such a silence between her parents that it had to be filled with conversations in her head. An only child, she had invented a brother on whom she fathered jokes.

Her mother had been what was then known as 'A Beauty', a category from whom presumably nothing further had ever been required. Certainly all the time that Margaret had known her the smallest demand from life had startled her into a dull, wordless fright. She flitted about the semi-dark of the passages as though fearful she might be trapped and eaten on the way. She fled, soundless except for the rustle of her dress, from one square box in the house to the next, closing each door silently behind her, holding the knob to prevent the click of the catch sometimes for a full minute so that it finally settled into place, horribly, when one had forgotten her, thought of her as already on the other side of the house.

The General, her father, was invisible all day, occupied with his automatic writing. Why were retired military men so often mystically sentimental? She had tried (unencouraged by him) to take an interest in this. But when a dog of theirs that had recently passed on – a tattered hearth-rug of a Scottie who had never done anything but eat noisily and sleep stinkily (in the drawing room in the evening he broke wind constantly and they had to pretend they did not hear, or notice the dreadful smells that swirled up towards them), when she discovered he was receiving spirit messages from Shag, messages of spiritual encouragement what is more (that self-obsessed, dim-bulb creature; if only he had said something characteristic, like 'God is sleep'), she decided to leave her father and his preoccupations alone. Not that he had noticed her interest.

At meal times they sat in unbroken quiet except for the clock which, like all the other clocks in the house (there were many) ticked slow and loud, inexorably emphasizing the empty silence: her mother glancing up from her food, her eyes, still beautiful, violet-coloured, looking nowhere in particular, but vaguely remembering it was impolite to concentrate too intently on her plate; her father chewing grimly (counting perhaps) his white moustache swivelling, with its inverted vee of nicotine stain. When she was a little girl she had thought this stain was rust, and her father made of iron, the rust soaking inward, his insides growing as yellow as his moustache. Once or twice, later, during the war, she met members of his old Corps. It appeared he had always been on detachment, organizing the feeding of coolies and so on; no one remembered anything of him.

Bryn Celyn was the Welsh name of this Scottish house; grey Victorian (late), too tall for its width, built on a villa'd hillside, other similar houses screened from each other, or almost screened, by rising plateaux of laurel and rhododendron that seldom flowered and the sadder, quicker-growing conifers.

Was it really as bad as all that? Margaret searched her memory. Certainly the rare times a cousin came to stay, after the initial giggles and exchange of news in the bedroom, when they went down to the first meal (served by dark, grey Ellen whom Margaret suspected of being a witch) the cousin fell silent also, and there was no getting the joy back however they tried, and no visit was ever repeated.

But children accept anything; it was her world. As an adolescent she had abstracted herself from it, caught up in her own inevitable dreams. Indeed she was Emily Brontë, burning all the more fiercely for the surrounding cold. Then they died. Her mother first and three months later her father. Had he received messages from her? It seemed unlikely they would be able to communicate across the Beyond any more freely than they had across the table.

After her father's death, clearing up, she had to go into his room, the first time in her life. It was a dark brown place, as she had imagined, and in the grate (where from the state of the chimney no other fire had ever been lighted) she found a mess of charred papers with the free-ranging scribble on them, as though written with the left hand, that had characterized the spiritual orthography of Shag. But the words My beloved – they could not have come even from him. She dropped the pieces back into the grate and set a match to them; she did not want to read too much, find too appalling the contrast between these endearments and the glacial world her parents had built around them. Why had they chosen to do that? Had they been, she permitted herself to wonder, both a little cracked? Let them be. Let them rest.

Now it was wartime – just. She found herself, a dreamy twenty-one, inheritor of three thousand pounds (the house she discovered not to be theirs but leased and no one wanted the huge dark furniture and the bronze effigies of snarling oriental animals that had frightened her mother so much. She paid a man to take them away). How empty she had felt, and cold. She might never have lived in the house she watched being dismantled. Let it go! Let my life begin! She went to London.

She shared a flat near the river, in Hammersmith, with a cousin called Dorothy. Two years older than Margaret, she was something at the Admiralty and was already immersed in the new exciting rhythms of wartime London. She was thin and small-boned, with the large strange-coloured eyes of Margaret's mother, but in her face they did not appear to swim, rather did they pounce from point to point, anxiously; to Margaret it was another proof of the mysterious, hair-line quality of beauty that Dorothy's eyes, so far as she could judge identical to her mother's, were so very different and not beautiful at all. But Dorothy could look very pretty in a fragile way. She wore her hair in a tightly permed bob, like an ATS girl, and much make-up, her mouth a dark slash. She found 1939 London thrilling, all the drama of farewells to 'boy-friends' (a favourite word of hers) that seemed to prolong themselves as everyone waited almost impatiently for the real war to begin; the sense of anticlimax drowned by noisy parties in blacked-out night-clubs, strangers immediately on Christian name terms, the social strata crumbling, the parties snowballing, smudgy kisses in boarded-up doorways, in the back of rare taxis, the sublimely different *difficulty* of everything, darkness, sandbags everywhere, the park torn up for gun-emplacements, ration-cards, gas-masks, good-byes. Nearly thirty years later Margaret could only think of Dorothy as a period figure, even her name brought back the rubber gas-mask smell and the bump at your side of the square cardboard box on a string that you had to carry it in, 'Put that light out!' and windows criss-crossed with brown sticky paper. The 'boy-friends' that Dorothy allowed to call for her (it was her name for any male of whatever age with whom she or Margaret were on speaking terms) were hardly boys. Portly men for the most part, with thinning hair. Only one did Margaret remember, because he stood so oddly. Making a joke, waiting for Dorothy as all her squires had to, he began very excessively to laugh and then she saw the reason for his strange stance – back hollowed, arms hanging away from his sides like a gorilla's – he had been holding in his paunch. He was a symbol for her of that time. What she chiefly remembered from this period of Dorothy's ceaseless flitting about, of the people she met through her, was an appalling, hopeless depression; not only at the dreadfulness of the war that must surely start properly soon, but at the dreadful, insupportable vulgarity it seemed to have stirred up.

She read a little, walked by the river, and tiring of that found herself a war-job at the Ministry of Food. It was there she learned to type. Not long after this she met Peter Forbes. Shy, unformed, a year younger than she was, they were well suited to learn from each other. She found him lost on her way home to Hammersmith one night in the black-out, his torch had broken; he was living quite near, waiting to be sent to learn to fly. They met in teashops and walked together by the river after his sporadic bouts of training (he learned drill while he waited, with a wooden cut-out for a rifle), he was lonely as she was, his old parents lived in the country, and then they made love in the flat while Dorothy was out. A few days afterwards he went to join his training squadron in Scotland, where he was killed immediately on a motor-cycle.

Even at the time, to Margaret, (perhaps to them both), it had seemed like a rehearsal, as though they were practising on each other, not cold-bloodedly, but because that was all they had in them so far to be able to do. Even her grief, which she gave way to, regarding herself as a war-widow, even that she had known in a part of herself was only a preliminary try-out of feelings that might one day really reach her. But she had been very miserable.

Then she met an older man, married, with two young children. He worked in her Ministry, in the propaganda department, a writer, handsome, much discussed among the girls. She discovered he was quite well known, she had even read some of his work. He came and sat by her one day in the canteen. She was flattered; she knew that some men found her attractive, but it always took her by surprise. She also knew that she had wanted him to notice her. Soon she was telling him about Peter Forbes. He was also called Peter and later he signed all his notes to her Peter Two, it was their name for him. The way she drank in his understanding made her realize how much she had needed it. Her love for him seemed to grow out of her feeling for her first Peter, not a betrayal but a continuation enlarged. Soon there was between them an intensity that spilled over the whole of drab, waiting London.

The end of the story was in the beginning; his situation. He became evasive, unhappy, made promises (to leave his wife, Margaret was his only love, etc.). He had meant them, twenty-five years later she was still certain of that. But nothing happened, except the bombing. There was always that excuse for putting things off, the public drama could be used to overdramatize the personal one. Despairing, she met his wife secretly. That was awful; not only because they liked each other but because they discovered each was being deceived in the same way, being given identical promises, they almost held hands like fellow victims.

Then she understood. He was watching them both, hoping to have the responsibility taken from him; she saw that he lay in his own indecisiveness like a warm bath, waiting for one of his women to lever him out, it didn't much matter which. She could have forgiven him anything but that. At first she could not quite believe it, then she did and her love died. It was as though he had cut at the very roots of sex in her. He had been insufficiently different, insufficiently a man after all. Years later she read his autobiography. Eventually he had left his wife and married someone else altogether, but his veiled reference to those days showed she had been right. The episode was described in terms of his guilt, his pain. In spite of his marvellous face, tenderness, intelligence, he had remained a baby.

He moved to another Ministry. Whether intentionally or not she never knew; the world was increasingly fluid in those days. Now London was even drabber than it had been before, unbearably so. Now she did suffer. She felt cold and ill.

The nights were full of violence and a kind of heroism disgusting to her. She felt that people had no right to be so long-suffering, scrawl 'business as usual' on their broken shops, 'Britain can take it'. Could it? She couldn't.

There was a personal violence as well, reflecting the other. Increasingly London was given over to a rootless sexuality. She let herself flow with it, there seemed no point in resisting. There was not much she could remember clearly, so meaningless it had all seemed. But she did remember the last – what? encounter? of that period – because she remembered her terror. A man she despised gained a complete physical ascendancy over her. It was as though she experienced in her own body the poisons that were being turned loose in Europe. She loathed him, he itched with hatreds yet he obsessed her. Somehow she found the strength to break it off, she thought he might kill her; she refused to answer the telephone or the door. She lay on her bed, her body aching, craving for him. It was horrible. A new kind of pain. She had not known the world contained so many.

She was ill after that for a long time, barely able to drag herself out of bed to the little kitchen to prepare herself some food. Dorothy did what she could when she was there, impatiently; she could never forgive Margaret for what she thought of as her success.

Margaret smiled, thinking of her as she took their breakfast cups back to the kitchen and rinsed out Charles's breakfast bowl. Dorothy became a little harder, a degree less excited as the months passed. The war had been both a high-point and a let-down. She had never married. Now she ran a typing bureau in Haywards Heath, rather gruffly, with her constant air of urgency still, and a large dog. Strange how the emancipation of women is so firmly tethered to the typewriter.

It was during this illness that Margaret had begun to read. When she could bear to go out again she joined the Left Book Club, the Fabian Society, went to lunchtime concerts at the National Gallery, consciously trying to rescue her life.

One day at the National Gallery she met Charles. He gave her a sandwich. It was typical of Charles that they were good sandwiches, the bread new ('fresh' was not a word to use about the strange wartime bread), spam, mustard, and that he had made them himself. He also had a bar of Victory chocolate in his pocket (had there been sawdust in wartime chocolate? – the taste was unmistakable surely?). It became a ritual. Each time she went he found her and they shared his lunch. They discussed the sandwiches more than the music.

This went on for perhaps a month, nothing else, just the music and the friendly sandwiches. Then one day he wasn't there and she found herself looking round, turning in her seat, examining the press that leaned against the walls or squatted on the floor in front of the dais and on the dais itself. Then she saw him, squeezed perilously near the soloist, almost among the pedals of the piano. He discreetly patted his pocket where the sandwiches were; he had been watching her look round for him.

He wore spectacles even then, had a large head broad at the top and covered with thinnish long brown hair that fell across his forehead in a straight diagonal. He was of course thinner but just as shapeless, although the tweed clothes that hung on him were always set off with a dangling coloured handkerchief in his breast pocket, a carefully chosen tie, as though he was consciously cultivating a style. This amused Margaret and pleased her. She had found that men who ignored their personal appearance were either dauntingly self-involved or, at best, unaware of women to the point of incomprehension. Behind his spectacles his round blue eyes looked at her, full of plans, not calculating but thinking, as though he was a man who knew what he wanted and would probably find some way to get it. After a while she became aware, although with no pressure at all, that he wanted her. She was glad.

Remembering Peter Two, she was dismayed to find that he was a writer, or at least that he had published 'verses' as he insisted on calling them, in *The London Mercury* before the war. He was proud of this but confessed, to her relief, that he did not regard himself as much of a talent; a critic perhaps, or better still, an editor. He was in his early thirties, perhaps seven or eight years older than she was (eight, she discovered; he had been thirty-two in the National Gallery days, she twenty-four) and Margaret had never met anyone with so few illusions about himself. He seemed almost to boast about the smallness of his gifts and the attainable nature of his ambitions. The services had turned him down because of his eyes; he worked in Government publishing and so, after the war, publishing perhaps? It all seemed too easy and might have been funny, perhaps Charles partly intended it to be, if it had not also been so marvellously sane in the middle of such a time. It was exactly what Margaret needed, a sense of order, an absence of strain.

There were also Charles's politics to give a dimension of seriousness. He took her to meet his Communist friends whom on the whole she liked. But she soon realized she would never make a Party member. At every point where she wanted to say 'But' she was required to make an act of faith hardly dissimilar from those her Catholic acquaintances boasted about. And Charles? Any scepticism he may have felt barely troubled him. He was aware of social injustice (his father, astonishing when one looked at the sedentary, entirely middle-class Charles, had been a miner), he could see no cure without a fundamental change. His own opinions were subservient to that. The Party was the most powerful instrument of social change, therefore it had his support. He worked very hard for it.

To Margaret it was as if ordinary daylight was returning. There were none of the lightning flashes, the warm, jungle shadows she had known with her second Peter. It was practical, steady, noon-light. It had never occurred to her that she was giving anything up by marrying Charles (for early on she decided that was what she would do) that she was 'settling' for anything. There are so many different kinds of marriage. The sort she wanted was one that would set her free, not put her on an emotional rack (never again!), give her scope to develop in her own way but not alone. This she had found with Charles. A selfish idea? She had never seriously regretted it. At twenty-four, she had been right about what she needed; as so often we are right about ourselves, she thought, if only we listen and don't force.

True it had been without passion. But she had not been a child. Physically it had always been successful because they learned each other very quickly when the time came, and soon moved inside the sexuality of the other happily, with an immediate tenderness that could rise without fierceness into something a little more. She had been lucky.

She frowned at the mirror in the dark hall, adjusting a scarf round her head before going out. Lucky. The word had a touch of smugness. Had her life been too easy? It was the peculiarity of our time to ask such questions, a real progress of a sort, a terror of narrowness; but she could not really *feel* such questions, and could not delude herself that restlessness signified a deeper response to life than content. She was lucky to be alive and not deadened by routine, busyness or affliction. Who would willingly seek the last of these? Who but the afraid allow themselves to be borne down by the first two? She had savoured her life and she wished to go on doing that. Her life lived in her, she felt it, and that was the only way she could understand it; in terms of awareness of herself, and through that, of others.

She was glad the mirror was dark, she had no wish to be unnecessarily dismayed by her appearance. But she continued to frown for another reason: she wondered if she had begun to drift lately. That was always a danger in her kind of quasi-solitary life. She had a horror of moving too far away from the everyday, of becoming a smiling freak, wearing odd clothes, talking to herself. She must take note of what other women were dressed in. She would buy some of the lastest beach-things for the holiday. Her forty-eight-year-old body (forty-eight!) had stood up pretty well so far, the outside of it anyway, and she would do it justice. Make old Charles's eyes glisten. Good. That was decided. The headscarf was perhaps too 1940, too Royal Family? It was cold outside and she had no hat. It would do. So she went, slowly, she was afraid of the return of those old stabbing pains round her heart, to do some shopping, to buy some clothes for the holiday and some food for their supper.

6

Charles climbed aboard his bus in London in a state of pleasurable indignation at the review of Jack Kerouac in a *New Statesman* he had picked up at Waterloo. First he was chidden for not having written a different book, then he was accused of being sentimental. As if sentimentality was not the risk that Kerouac chose to take – the risk of all such diffuse, affirmative writing! Sometimes he was, certainly, but intellectual England seemed to Charles dominated by twin fears, the fear of sentimentality and the fear of priggishness. Comfortable critics inverted their sentimentality to invoke a poetry of violence, pundits on television said 'fuck' to show they were not middle aged. Meanwhile troops of the young who do not listen and who do not swear, unnoticed by critics, made a cult of gentleness, and painted their motor-cars with flowers. That blind old woman on the *Statesman*! But in America – where there is violence and few are sufficiently protected to have any sentimentality to invert – there were still men unselfconscious enough to take a risk or two, who could praise and weep in public, who did not care who laughed!

Hearing him mutter, seeing him move his head, the girl next to him half got up to let him out. A glance out of the window showed him that it was indeed his stop. He often went past it by mistake, enjoying the unexpected walk back. He thanked her and climbed down the stairs, putting his ticket in the box.

Entering his office building he greeted the lift-man, Bob, who was a surly customer he had been working on for years. They could only reach agreement on the unpleasantness of the weather. He had never been heard to agree with anyone on any other subject. On the rare indisputably perfect day Charles looked forward to his version of it. Too windy? Too close? His favourite had been on a morning of such champagne freshness the very paving-stones had seemed to refresh the feet. Charles carefully held his peace in the lift. Between the third and the fourth floor the strain of waiting for another cheeriness to snub had been too much for Bob. 'This weather!' he'd growled at his floor buttons. 'The girls better *watch it*!' His job was unnecessary and there was no quicker way to sour a man. They could have worked the lift themselves, it would also have been quicker, Bob had his own way of punishing the world. But he was employed by the building, not by Charles, who would have found him something more useful to do.

He admitted the difficulty of working out one's political responsibility except in terms of corporate action. The hat he took round for Bob at Christmas, secretly, bullying everyone, *that* was not the way.

Notwithstanding Bob, or perhaps relieved to get away from the problem he represented, Charles always closed himself into his office with a metaphorical rubbing of the hands. There were problems here he *could* solve – and not too many. There was also Norman near at hand – no, not today, it was Norman's day off. Pity.

Norman professed himself the follower of a man called Tales, an Alexandrian who had taught that all emotion was foolish, even sympathy, and the wise man was as little affected by the misfortunes of others as he was by his own. Charles was never sure just how serious Norman was. Perhaps completely. What was certain, and what fascinated Charles, was Norman's entire abandonment of the concept of the 'Nice'.

'Niceness' was a thread running through contemporary secular society, more or less holding it together. However far most men strayed on either side of it, the thread was always used for reference purposes. Even the most extravagant divagationists, those asocial elements whom the newspapers loved to call 'hell-raisers' – drunkards, scroungers, deceivers of friends, stealers of friend's wives, even these apostles of the dud cheque, beat their breasts in their sober moments or when they had been caught, castigating themslves for their departures, promising to keep nearer the Nice in future. None of them had the courage of the mousey, uncreative Rimbaud that was Norman, who had simply abandoned the concept altogether. Of course he was not 'Nasty'. That would not have been prudent in a Nice oriented society. He did his work as well as was necessary for the maintenance of his wages, cared nothing for the pain of others, refused to recognize his own, pursued bodily pleasure with detachment and received rebuffs with equanimity. Aesthetic matters were of no interest to him, nor were political or spiritual ones. He regarded the world as mad: his duty to remain the one sane man.

If Charles had written all his own views and prejudices on separate pieces of white card and laid them out on the floor to look at them, he knew that most would cancel each other out and some would qualify others into meaninglessness. Norman's would be few but neat, could be picked up from the floor in sequence and laid, clear-edged one upon the other. Amazing! Charles laughed. If he were the subordinate Norman would sack him. But it was Norman who was that, contented to be so, and the relative powerlessness of his tidier cards comforted Charles.

There was no doubt, however, that the Nice could do with continual overhaul. Although we could hardly live without it, the frequent shocks that Norman gave Charles he regarded as an invaluable therapy.

For example: his girl before last had announced to Norman that she was pregnant. That day Norman had drawn from the bank a sum sufficient for an abortion and two months' modest keep. In an envelope he had given this to the girl together with the name of a good abortionist and told her that he wished never to see her again. Her protests (she was a Yugoslavian who wanted to settle in Britain and use Norman as a basis for a new and probably Norman-less life) were useless, so were her tricks, some of them brilliant. Norman simply forgot her.

Why did Charles find such behaviour shocking? For the interest of the conundrum he was grateful to Norman. There are so many meaningless genuflections in the direction of the decent that Norman's simple coolness had an economy about it. Wherein was it false? Would it have been better for Norman to consult his friends, be publicly and privately self-tortured and in the end do exactly the same thing? Worry more at first, forget her at last, but after a long period? Why?

Norman's presence, only his feet visible most of the day, was Charles's equivalent, in his tiny kingdom, of the Court Jester, keeping him awake. As is the case with all the best jesters he was never quite sure which of them was the more foolish.

He settled down to work through his In-tray, gratifyingly full of interdepartmental memos, a game he enjoyed playing. There were also several new first novels, this year he was a member of a prize-giving panel. A pleasant day of reading stretched ahead, if there was nothing troublesome among all this. He left a long memo from Colm until the last. It was the fruit of his suggestions last week, Colm obediently asking for assistance in his music department. As usual he made too many verbal jokes, the style a mixture of the flippant and the departmental that didn't come off, his unease showed. Charles spent half an hour pencilling in his corrections. That should do the trick. He sent it off to be re-typed and rang for Colm to come down.

He was the latest in a line of people he had taken under his small wing. Once or twice, needing young blood for the music department, he had heard Colm's work mentioned, not always approvingly. He had listened to some of it and although not musical himself, he had sensed in it (witty, plaintive, violent by turns) a kind of impatience, a young man kicking to be let out of some prison, possibly of his own making. He sounded to Charles like someone who needed time; and time, for composers as for everbody, is money. He made inquiries. He lived by doing occasional musical scores for films, which made him sound too expensive, but Charles also discovered that he now taught and disliked that very much. They met.

Charles found him an attractive youngish man at an in-between stage. Too old now to live on youthful promise but by no means yet established. He seemed not very attracted to the job, probably imagining it would take too much of his time. Charles had no wish to spell out how little he would have to do – an occasional article that would be filed away in damp corners of the Commonwealth, edit a magazine of musical happenings culled from newspapers, perhaps an introductory programme note for a provincial concert – token activities, the job was a concealed subsidy for his own work, but that was for him to realize.

Charles was willing to throw a life-belt but it was up to Colm to catch it, Charles couldn't jump into the water as well. Colm asked time to think it over. Apparently his hatred of teaching had triumphed over his fear of an office job, because he accepted. Three days a week and eight-hundred a year. He was lucky. But it had not worked out altogether well. Like so many of his kind, used to intensive bouts of work for small reward, or none, he still could not believe he was paid so much to do so little. What he did was either slapdash or meticulous beyond all need. Charles had the impression that the office, intended merely to be a source of bread, was casting its shadow over his private working life. He sighed. Colm was not easy. Even his office clothes were obsessively subfusc and he looked bad in them. In the corridors he stood aside to let Charles pass in a parody of some imagined office protocol, making it clear that he regarded the whole set-up a charade. Artists protected themselves in many ways; better the usual aggressive flamboyance than this punctilious detachment. Better for Colm.

His knock came at the door. He'd try to talk to him.

'Enter!'

Colm didn't exactly sidle in, but he wore his subaltern air, learned presumably during some period of National Service. It suited his tall figure and large intelligent head (hair unbecomingly tidy) not in the least, and Charles could see why some people, Norman among them, were uneasy in his disguised watching presence. He behaved unnaturally because he thought others expected it. A subtle and probably unintentional rudeness.

'Just the job that memo of yours. You won't mind if I change the phrasing slightly, will you? I'll let you see it before I pass it on.'

'Don't bother. I'm sure you'll improve it. Difficult to hit the right note.... How's your wife?'

'In need of a holiday. As we all are.' Charles turned his smiling face on Colm, he guessed it was the sort of remark that irritated him.

Colm walked to the window, stared out. Charles wondered if

he knew how clearly his movement had said 'Save me from this over-cosy buffer!' He doubted it.

'You don't feel in need of one yourself?'

Colm turned. 'You know I'm *not* overworked, don't you?'

'The term is a wide one. Your work is music. How's it going?'

'Not well.'

'Colm – it's only a small toad you have to swallow. Don't strain on it. Your job isn't much, but it's useful. Use it to give yourself scope.'

'But I don't want to regard myself as a special case.'

'Maybe you aren't.'

Colm laughed. 'I don't know about that!'

'Anyway – rubbish!' It was Charles's turn to move, Colm's shape in the window was dazzling him, he left his desk and went over, sighing again. (Have we the right to infect the young with our middle-aged resignations? Have they the right to demand understanding from us, who are only one stumble further on than they are?) But, oddly, there was nothing tiresome about Colm; only a disinclination to play certain games. He was now trying to respond to a situation that was after all not of his making. Charles had a sudden flash of insight; what if Colm's prickliness, surprising in one so obviously able to look after himself, what if his whole difficulty arose from an exaggerated loyalty to him, Charles – from affection even? As soon as he had the thought he knew there was truth in it. Colm was actually fond of him.

He went and stood by him at the window, both of them looking out at the sad confusion of the London skyline.

'When my son was born the nearest I got to prayer ever, I think, was to the genes not to combine in any form that added up to a special gift. . . . My prayer was answered.'

Colm didn't know whether to laugh. He knew Charles had had a son who was now dead. His face gave no clue.

Now he made a gesture towards the view they both looked at.

'How would you feel about this if you were a good architect?'

'Sick.'

'Would that be a reason for giving up architecture?'

Colm feared that Charles was going to say something holy about the Artist. He had a way of talking about them as though they were some kind of First Eleven – Pick Your Own World Team; desperately, it was crude but anything to stop him, he said, 'Have you seen the papers this morning?'

'Yes.' Good. He was on the right track with this young man. (There was news that the entire population of a Vietnamese village had been burned to death by mistake. The Americans were offering compensation at the rate of two hundred dollars per head. To deal with such matters he had a jargon he believed in.) 'Yes. I saw. What would you do? Stop the war? Of course. Change the politicians? You can't. Join protest movements? Hunger strikes? Why not? Better to protest than do nothing. But isn't it more difficult to leave the relatively unambiguous action to those who have a call for it, who will anyway be better at it than you are, and for you to do the one thing you can do and they can't, sit alone in your room, hyenas of selfishness howling all round you, and write music?'

For Colm the writing of music was not an activity that took place in a vacuum, but Charles either understood that or he didn't. He probably did – words are blunt instruments. 'The Tai-phong Requiem with hyena accompaniment?'

'Oh ... who will ever paint Guernica again? Faith in such immediate connections has died in all of us. But against the huge negative you still have to put your small positive. The knowledge of its smallness may be the biggest load your vanity has to bear.' He paused, he wanted that to go home. 'It is only by accepting the hugeness of the negative you can do any work of value. The more you feel it the smaller will seem your positive contribution. To pretend your work is *more* important, for its own sake, is the kind of selfishness that kills. But there is another kind – really we need another word – the kind that says: I see, I feel and I can do nothing direct, but this I can do and I shall.'

True, so far as it went. Like most generalizations it flattered itself, assuming that by stating the problem you came near solving it. On the other hand, what Findus was saying was more interesting in its sound than its content. Colm found this about most human communications, he derived more information from tone than he did from words. So often words were interchangeable or belonged to other people; father, schoolmaster, favourite author – the way they were said was what one should really listen to. And he was touched by the way Findus had said all this, as though to himself, presumably wanting to help. He had moved about the room, a little sightlessly, and now he dropped himself behind his desk again, took off his spectacles with one hand and rubbed his eyes with the thumb and forefinger of the other, making them look red and old.

'Oddly enough, they understood these things better in the nineteenth century,' he said. 'It's all very obvious of course. It could be used as an argument for withdrawal. . . . In the end,' he looked bewildered and slightly winded, 'such decisions are private, moral ones.' He sounded disappointed. He put his spectacles back on and looked at Colm. 'Really, I don't know why I tire myself out telling you things you already know. How else can one think of these dreadful matters?'

Colm was distressed by this sudden deflation; ashamed of the impatience he must have let Findus notice.

'No other way, I think.'

Charles certainly had depressed himself. 'When you find things – ah – getting you down, what do you do?'

'Have dreams of flying.'

'Really?' . . . His own dream life, however princely, was comfortingly earth-bound.

'Yes. I just take off, float round ceilings and things. It's so vivid that when I wake up I'm certain for a time I could still do it. I look down on everyone.'

'Contemptuously?'

'Not a bit. In dreams one doesn't seem to need that amount of compensation. No, I just float and look down with a kind of warm, mild interest. Feel free.'

'How splendid!'

'In fact, I've taken up gliding to see if it can repeat the sensation.'

'How very literal-minded of you. Does it?'

'Not at all.'

They both smiled. Charles was glad he'd tried to be an uncle because he saw that Colm was glad, too.

'Well, I suppose we'd better get on with our clock-watching. Try not to despise yourself too much – it's only conceit.'

'That's exactly what it is.'

'And don't get too un-conceited, will you.'

'Not a chance.'

Quite successful, Charles thought, when Colm had gone. But he had spoken the truth when he said he felt tired. Talking to people younger than oneself was always tiring, one never knew what part of them their youth made deaf. It was like screwing oneself up to howl the obvious down an ear-trumpet that was only partially and unpredictably blocked. But long ago he had decided never to be afraid of the deafeningly obvious, it is always news to somebody.

The telephone had been marvellously silent this morning and remained so. He looked at his watch: 12.15; the time people began to ring each other up in a belated attempt to justify their morning. They did the same thing around quarter past five – the clockwork of office life driven by guilt. He'd escape the lunch-time flurry if he left the office now, had a quiet sandwich while he glanced at a couple of those novels, and then did something he'd been promising himself for ages – visit Norman at home; have a look at his new domestic set-up; he'd have something to tell Margaret. Having decided this, he could hardly wait. 'Back at four,' he called to his secretary. 'Put any calls through to Mr Treacey, we might as well make him work for his living,' and to avoid the sometimes infectious gloom of Bob he quickly walked down the stairs into the, to him, bus-and-shopfront-glorious Holborn, air the colour of brass bedsteads in the fume-filtered sun.

Norman lived up a flight of eighteenth-century stairs in Charlotte Street. In the old Fitzrovian days his flat had obviously been a studio but now the huge high room was partitioned into segments that stopped half-way to the ceiling, which gave the place an emergency appearance as though hastily converted by the Ministry of Works. One of the segments was a bathroom (the fittings ante-dating the partitions, perhaps, even, the house), another was a primitive kitchen, and so on. It was very nasty, largely because Norman (and whoever was his consort of the moment) never opened the windows. These were anyway on the street side and partly partitioned off – they grimly illuminated two little cubicles, one of which Norman used for his 'papers' (that's to say anything he wasn't using) and the other was stuffed with objects left behind by previous occupants, buckets, rags, a chair leaking springs and sawdust and the unwieldily rusting remains of a huge stove and its chimney that had presumably been the atelier heating in the days of Nina Hamnett. Norman (and consort) lived, slept and ate in the large first segment whose door opened directly on to the landing. In the absence of windows it was lit by a large skylight still with hefty remains of green black-out paint on it, causing a dim, unequal crepuscule rather like that of certain railway stations.

Charles, standing on the linoleum of the landing patterned to resemble parquet, knocked on the door and hearing no reply opened it. He was immediately assaulted by a heavy, damp, white object, difficult to disentangle from, which he found to be a sheet. There was another hung on a string across the room, cutting it into two triangles and in one of these was the bed, close to the floor, and in the bed was Olga sitting up and glowering at him, a green overcoat lengthways over her shoulders like a cumbersome scarf.

'Olga?' said Charles adjusting his spectacles, disturbed in the struggle. 'I'm so sorry – Charles Findus – I didn't hear a reply to my knock – so I –' he gestured to the door, smiling. She continued to glare.

'Through,' she said, pointing at the dripping curtain. Newspapers spread inaccurately underneath it caught some of the wet and a slight fog came from it, caused by two electric fires on their backs beamed up at the sheets; wisps like march-mist eddied a few inches up towards the skylight, but the draughts up there discouraged them at once, they curled down quickly and disappeared, becoming merely a damp smell. The whole process was illuminated by a naked central bulb of extreme brightness.

Charles, following the direction of her pointing finger, pushed through the sheet and came upon the figure of Norman almost invisible as he peered deep into the bowels of a very white, inappropriately modern washing-machine.

'I see how it functions.' His voice boomed inside. 'Most ingenious.'

'Wash-day?' said Charles.

Norman withdrew his head and turned. 'Ah.... Really very clever.'

'What are you two men whispering about?' yelled Olga. They pushed back, stepping over the fires, and pulled up chairs next to her bed, Charles at the foot and Norman at the head, where she had to turn awkwardly to see him. Charles had often noticed how difficult Norman found it to station himself appropriately in relation to either objects or people, as though positions in space presented no pattern that he could see; he created awkward angles which after a while became extremely irritating, but he was unaware of this.

'Olga has a condition,' he smiled. 'Would you like some tea?'

'No, thank you.'

He had noticed Norman's drying socks through the door of the cubicle kitchen pinned to the draining-board by cups.

Norman must have had a very secure childhood not to feel threatened by such chaos. Winchester and New College. It was only on such a basis of order that this kind of disorder could stand. His own terror of the slum-like stemmed from its childhood nearness, the battles his mother had fought. Norman had enough money to sweep all this away – he could have *moved* for heaven's sake! Charles decided not to blame himself for his squeamishness.

Just then Olga gave a bass cry and leapt with extreme urgency out of the bed towards Charles, revealing as she did so quantities of thigh, and more, and quantities of breast also. She galloped to the door. The lavatory was on the landing, he was relieved to remember.

He and Norman sat in silence for a moment.

'Something she ate.'

'Ah.'

'A curry.'

'Did you eat it too?'

'Oh yes.'

No need to ask if *he* was all right. Charles could not resist glancing towards the sheets, still wisping away, the damp seemed to be settling round their ankles.

'An accident last night. We borrowed that machine. Marvellous thing.'

They fell silent again, Charles contemplating the tousled sheetless bed, Norman's old-mended pyjamas, the dented pillows pulled towards the centre. He censored a vision of Norman's thin shanks quivering – it was too unfair – how would he like someone to imagine him like that? Not that it was shameful. But even Diogenes, he remembered, who rejected all shame, only tried it once in public and then abandoned the idea. It was a private act, the privacy a part of it. What about those shameless photographs? Why had he kept them? There must be (there *were*) pockets of juvenile lust wisping up from secret depressions in the landscape of his manhood – pocked like the surface of the moon. So foolish. And in his head. Norman played out his fantasies on real flesh whereas he – twenty-four years with Margaret, settled, rhythmic, swaddled by his pleasure in her, believing in the socialist millennium – where would he stand when that millennium struck, allowing himself such little leaky day-dreams? Norman took his pleasures in the here and now, believing in no future at all. Charles watched the little puffs of steam coming off the sheets, warm, rising as they must towards the cold, faltering, and then becoming invisible. Again they sat in silence while the cistern flushed on the landing.

Olga returned explosively, groaning, threw herself on the bed and stared at the ceiling as though in fierce prayer. Then she leaned forward and began to hiss at Norman, very intensely.

'You're so *mean*! Oh Olga we must go to the Taj Mahal, it's so *cheap*! So *cheap* – it's all he ever says – *cheap* – like a little bird in a cage! So he poisons me with cat-meat and then it's bedtime and Oh *nice* Olga and let me do this Olga and you do that Olga oh darling Olga. . . . It's *disgusting*!' She shouted this last and threw herself back on the bed, communing again with the roof.

It had been mostly addressed to Charles, but was not embarrassing partly because of Norman's lack of reaction, partly because the whole cut of Olga proclaimed a girl who found such importunities the opposite of disgusting and also because she spoiled her case by going on:

'You know he dreams of other women? Oh, I can tell. He wakes up with his little smile – you see, his little smile? Filthy dreamer! Filthy things! Here am I warm and loving, a woman! And he dreams of his little things!' Clearly Norman had heard it all before. She was letting off steam, like the sheets. Charles, who had never been able to make love with any pleasure to someone he did not like, and he found Olga unarguably dreadful, wondered again at the detachment of Norman. But he suspected that Olga would have the same mechanistic attitude to sex. A good arrangement in fact if you could put up with the boredom. Boredom, of course, put you in a position of power, kept you safe. Norman now gave her a peck on the forehead which she endured, and the two men pushed again through the sheets towards the large work-table, covered with papers and books.

'Stop talking smut you two!' yelled Olga.

'Splendid girl,' said Norman. He indicated the table. 'The Simonides.'

Charles waited.

'One of the Sunday's is going to run it. "The Man and his Millions."'

That Simonides ... Charles had vaguely registered his name; one of the innumerable shipping millionaires.

'They're printing 50,000 first impression.'

'My dear Norman! How marvellous! Lawrence's must be thrilled.' This was the small publishing house that had been printing Norman with small profit to themselves for fifteen years.

'Acropolis are doing it.' (A huge concern specializing in the memoirs of retired statesmen.) 'Lawrence's couldn't match their advance.'

Lawrence's ditched, therefore? Practical. Sentiment has no place in such transactions. Can we live without it?

'Is he of interest?'

'Not at all.'

'What's he like?'

'Extremely unhappy.'

'Money isn't everything?'

'He's impotent.'

Charles roared with laughter. Norman writing this book, the clearly insatiable Olga waiting –

'Some filthy joke!' she yelled from behind the curtain.

'Charles thinks it's funny that Simonides is impotent,' Norman called back, mildly.

'No –' objected Charles, but he was interrupted by Olga.

'Nonsense – he prefers little boys. Like all you men.'

'Does he?' murmured Charles.

'He didn't mention it. We went quite thoroughly into the matter. He's tried glandular treatment. Without success. He's now installed a contraption for hanging himself, something to do with freeing the spinal cord. We both tried that. Quite effective.' Charles was having difficulty controlling his face. 'Olga, however, thinks we all really want choir-boys. I encourage her in this delusion. It makes her correspondingly grateful.' He began to laugh himself now, silently, his bottom jaw yawing up and down, his head slightly tilted back. They returned to Olga.

'What have you two been *doing* to each other,' she shouted, eyes narrowed. Charles turned his delighted gasp into a small movement, 'I really must be going.' (He must memorize all this for Margaret.) He left them sitting on the bed holding hands, looking at him, and as he went down the stairs he found himself, as always after a session with Norman, amazingly cheered up.

'He's so *dismal*, Charles,' Margaret used to complain in the early days when they both saw more of him; she was wrong.

There comes a time when men's hearts sink utterly, they understand at last that friendships fade beyond repair, that girls die, that our wars bring nothing about, our lovers are all untrue. The cold indifference of life tugs at them like a dirty wind and they taste their own futile deaths. For a moment there is nothing. Some kill themselves. Others (often writers) spend their lives proclaiming nothing as though it is their private discovery, calling the world complacent because it won't listen. The world already knows. Most of us tuck the chill more or less out of sight.

Not Norman. He began from the chill, his thin hair-like roots were put down an inch or two into the stony rubbish itself. No wind could freeze him further, he lived at wind temperature. To Charles it was a kind of triumph that man could survive – anyway Norman could – on bread alone. He even considered the possibility that Norman might be some kind of secular saint. St Anthony, St Jerome, they had lived in caves for a purpose, but Norman's Thebaid had no purpose at all and he faced its desolation with a perfect calm. Charles had so many pillows. So had Margaret – different ones. Colm's angularities were those of a man punching different pillows until he found one that didn't collapse in a shower of choking feathers. But Norman's pillow was a stone, and he always found somebody to share it. True they usually became indignant when they discovered just how hard it was.

Privately he considered Norman's views rubbish. Colm was right to go on angrily testing for a true comfort. What he admired about Norman was the perfection of his lack of faith. Margaret could never understand this. To her Norman had simply failed to become a human being. But the difference between those who believe in something greater than themselves and those who don't is not a difference in quality, a separation between the first- and second-rate (whichever way round you put it). What matters is the way a man applies his discoveries to his life. Most of us think one way and live another, shuttling between varieties of confusion. The mystery-mongers had fallen quite rightly into disrepute because when they reached a difficulty they produced a god or a miracle – Graham Greene did this – the last card up their sleeve. Norman did not cheat in that way. In spite of the disorder he lived among there was really a kind of machine-like precision in his life, and no wastage.

It was mid-afternoon now and Charles caught a bus, pleasantly empty at this time of day. There was only one other person on the top deck, a girl, sitting on one of the front seats. As Charles made his way towards the other front seat he had time to appraise her hair, the kind he particularly liked – grey-gold, with no sign of the hairdresser, straight but not limp, springing softly as she moved her head. As he sat down he turned to see the face in front of the hair, prepared to be disappointed, but he wasn't. On the contrary, it was seldom nowadays (it had always been seldom) he saw the type of face to which he had addressed his youthful dreams. Archaic, simple, a face to go on Quests because of, before which to make Firm Purposes of Amendment ... how mysterious that was! The head balanced unfussily on the neck like a Greek khora, and round the corners of the large mouth there were traces of that ancient half-conscious half-smile – although at that moment she looked very serious. He could stare all he wished because she was wholly involved in writing something in a large notebook, the tip of her tongue moving, as though she was unaccustomed to such effort. Occasionally she lifted her eyes (grey-green Charles saw) and stared in front of her, doing that wonderful thing he loved in a face above all else: when she moved her eyes she moved her head as well. Margaret did that. It was a movement of utter frankness, without irony or self-protection. Where was the place in Norman's cosmology for girls like this and the (doubtless) foolish dreams that they inspire?

She cupped her cheek and chin in her hand and turned away to stare out of the window. The notebook lay on her knee; the handwriting was large and round and Charles was able to read what she had written. *Reasons for not being unfaithful to Simon.*

Charles sighed. The daughters of Beauty are no different from the rest of us. Such a sublunary dilemma! And yet ... Life offered no special protection to such a creature. Utterly wrong if it did. To think that life had to become special to contain her was to insult life, the confusion of an old sentimentalist; he rebuked himself. If the delicate was unable of its own strength to survive then it had no right to and Norman was justified. Let her life be as triangular as need be! May she – he now addressed the Processes of History – make the right decision! Was such marvellousness meant for only one man? Perhaps. He had known that strange thing. If not; let her make her decision and live! He almost chanted this aloud, seeing his stop approaching, getting excited. He got up and saw beneath the heading '(i) *Because I know him better than anyone else in the world.*' Things didn't look too good for Simon. There was also a (ii) but he couldn't read that. The rest of the page was blank. May she know others as well as she knew Simon! May she rest those eyes on the souls of others and still be able to love them. May she find the one (a big prayer this) who can recognize her and nevertheless resist the terrible impulse to spoil! ... In an elevated state he got off the bus. He refused to feel ashamed of himself. Because such beings are rare (he addressed the bell-push of the lift now) is that a reason to check one's excitement in their presence? Dreams could be a form of damp-rot, undermining social progress, certainly, but those were false dreams of an easy escape. If you reform the basis of society there would be less necessity for these. Therefore the dreams that get themselves dreamed will be closer to reality, will they not? He believed Yes – it was certainly worth a try. Meanwhile to proscribe all dreaming was not only bigoted, it was impossible.

The lift arrived with Bob, always at his worst around four o'clock.

'How are you?' said Charles automatically, preoccupied, stepping into the lift.

'Overworked and underpaid,' said Bob, equally automatically.

Yes. If for 'worked' you substituted 'bored' that was perfectly true. The penalties for inflicting demoralizing repetitive tasks on a fellow human would be very severe in Charles's Commonwealth. The trouble is that jobs makyth man and Charles knew that Bob, whatever task he was given now, would always consider himself exploited. That was only partly Bob's fault, but Charles refused to feel sorry for him, he'd as soon have thought of punching him, or giving him a kiss.

He remembered his father's contempt for a bad workman. Surely it was possible to be a good lift-man? No. That was a flabbily 'Christian' thought – basis for conscience-free exploitation – the rewards for the Just Servant being Hereafter (and costing nothing), lift-users needn't bother their heads about lift-operators. Somebody Else would take care of them.

His father.... How he had admired, how he had longed to get away from, that hard, narrow man. Well – he had done so. What had become of his Nottingham accent? Gone, like his hair and his waist. (When he had first met Margaret, although so much of that struggle lay in the past, how pleased he had been to discover that she was a General's daughter! Ashamed, he had salved his conscience by careful and continuous references to his working-class background. Little by little he had learned, almost by the way, of Margaret's dreadful childhood, so much more deprived than his own, and he had fallen silent, even more ashamed.) Perhaps (his inability to deal with Bob often reminded him of this), perhaps he should have stayed and involved himself further in the Labour movement as his father had wanted him to? He had no talent for it. Also he had yearned for what he then called 'wider horizons'. Perhaps he'd lacked the courage for that bitter necessary struggle. He'd certainly kept his eye on wider horizons than his father's, and that could not be bad. But now when he turned, three hundred and sixty degrees, they were still there but somehow imperceptibly shrunk; he was like a man on a stage in a pool of light, the beam narrows, the circle shrinks, the man begins to limit his movements, one step in any direction and he will disappear into the encroaching dark.

However, neither Bob nor he could be changed at this late date. It was the course of history that had to be altered, or rather, correctly followed. He had so much to be grateful for – a bromide, but true. He remained cheerful because cheerfulness had become the habit of his mind. He did not know that Bob, recognizing him, reserved for him a special dislike. If he had known he would have understood.

7

It was still spring in London, a fortunate one. Colm and Beatrix made the most of it. They met when they could, sometimes it was only briefly. Beatrix, although she gave herself up to this new emotion – and it was a new kind, the correspondences with the early Simon days were frequent but irrelevant, this was taking place in a different arena, one that was strange to her – privately she slowed herself down, pacing it, and sometimes she pretended she could only manage half an hour. This they would spend in a café, a park, anywhere, it didn't matter, then she would go home to be by herself, or with the children, sometimes finding Simon there, and she'd turn this new thing over in the part of herself where it seemed to live. Other times they would have a whole afternoon together, go boating on Regent's Park Lake, to the Zoo; they behaved like children, knowing they were not children, allowing it to sink to that level of themselves which would know when the time came, presumably, what it was they had to do.

Just as Beatrix purposely withdrew sometimes, pretending to be needed at home because her instinct told her to do this, Colm was unpressing, astonished, only once occluded by an anger that frightened them both because they both recognized its source. As they came closer they discovered a real terror, as though their private selves were being outraged; with the desire to let go there was also a need violently to hang on to their separateness, to hit out in defence of it, there was something black and pregnant with the possibility of hatred in this slow invasion of each other. The instinct to fight was strongest in Colm because he feared this assault on a self he had spent his life trying to keep intact. A part of Beatrix also cried out: Not yet – I'm not ready! But another side of herself always said: No. On.

They behaved like young lovers because they were young, but neither was as young as that. Each had a past which dictated the present slow pace. They were not playing with each other or at being in love (that delightful pastime) but playing, rather, around something in which they began dimly to guess their futures. Part of their pleasure was that they found themselves behaving like all the lovers they had ever seen or heard of: holding hands, suddenly running, laughing together at nothing, but they knew they would willingly pay the price of such innocence when the time came.

For Colm it was as though he was seeing another human face at last. A film seemed to peel off his own. He remembered a phrase of Bacon's, 'faces but a gallery of pictures – where there is no love'. For the first time he caught the glow of another separate existence as vivid to him as his own.

Beatrix loved the hard, shuttered side of Colm, loved the parts that were mysterious to her as much as the rest, perhaps more. But she rejoiced in the change in him because she knew she had caused it. His new softness was hers and she saw all that was happening to her written, daily, on his face.

The physical link between them was not pressing at first because there was so much else. It became tauter as time passed. They never went to Colm's flat, he never suggested it. As time went on she knew he had been right. He was listening, as she was. To both of them it seemed they were moving to some distant tune.

Once they spent an evening together. It wasn't a success. As the moment to separate approached, the thought became more and more absurd – had they been listening to the right music? – she could see the question settling on Colm like dust. It was then he had frightened them both, turned on her hard, trying to hurt, succeeding. He clearly willed himself to see her coldly, a girl he'd got involved with and the whole thing had become ridiculously overblown. She didn't feel love for him then, or non-love. It was like watching a struggle that was also hers. They parted coldly, didn't bother to arrange another meeting and she barely noticed. When they met the next day (Colm telephoned) neither referred to the previous night, but it was as though a pustule inside

Colm had burst, he was gentler than before, with an ever greater astonishment at the back of his eyes as if that bursting had surprised him by the strength of what it had failed to destroy.

So two weeks passed, three. A short time, but not for them.

Then, one evening, their first together after the bad one, although they'd met many times since and that was forgotten, Colm said: 'I want to go away with you.'

Beatrix felt as if her turn had come to jump from the aeroplane; she had been waiting for it but her first reaction, her stomach lurching, was – how far is the drop?

'A week-end somewhere?'

'Longer. Let's go abroad. I'm due a holiday. Two weeks.'

'Yes.'

It was time to say the next thing.

'Simon?' Colm made a small, helpless gesture. 'Shall I...?'

'No. Of course not. I must.'

'I can't bear to think of –'

'Ssh ... I'll tell him.' Surely Colm didn't expect her to comfort him?

There are not only poisons inside us, there are others outside as well. We have to drink a bit of them all. Make others drink.

Colm saw her withdraw. Until they got through this they couldn't go on and she had to do it on her own. It was a betrayal. That there was nothing he could do did not absolve him.

They left the restaurant and he took her home; their second bad parting, in silence. He felt the innocent sureness leaking away. To hell with it then. Innocence was no use unless it had been lost and re-won. They had always had to earn it, from the beginning.

She climbed the steps to her front door as though going to her execution and he left her there, feeling criminal, forbidding himself to feel any such thing.

All action contains a kind of murder – if only the death of the alternatives we did not choose. To put a nose out of doors is to disturb the air. Whatever there was between them, had always had this brutality among its roots. So be it. The roots must not be allowed to be poisoned by it.

He walked through the dark streets astonished again at the

cannibal nature of life – someone had to be eaten before they could be together. But he felt the cannibal part of himself triumphing whenever he remembered her lack of hesitation.

The streets became noticeably dingier as he walked from where she lived to where he did, which reminded him; economically Beatrix was in a different world. Had he been glamourized by that? No. But what part of her specialness derived from that dark money-soil? How much were the freely moving, noiseless wheels of their love greased by the knowledge that whatever the other problems, money wasn't one of them? It was her access to the stuff that made this possible.... No! To make finicking investigations into his motives was obscene! If it was her money that dazzled him he was reminded of the reply a dedicated lover of women had made when accused by some Freudian idiot of being a repressed homosexual. 'If I am,' he'd said, 'it's in an area inaccessible to introspection.'

He bought himself half a bottle of brandy at a pub, climbed the stairs to his flat, put on the electric fire and every light in the place, and poured himself out a half-tumbler. He put some Bartok unaccompanied violin on the pick-up and drank sitting on the arm of the chair. He was glad he'd never brought her to this place. The nervous music, apparently disjointed but not, soothed him. Other men had their confusions. They used them. He poured some more brandy. It was like passing the time while Beatrix had an operation – he had to stop himself ringing up to find out how it had gone. When they met tomorrow he'd be talking to a survivor, would never know what it had been like, and she would never forgive him for not being there. We are never any use to each other finally, there's a cleft between us never quite filled in; but you could grab hands across the cleft, hold on tight, but ... Christ! What if her talk with Simon had gone differently, she'd changed her mind, she'd let his hand go after all?

The force of that stopped him in the middle of the room like a bullet. The last doubts, if there were any left, if he hadn't been playing with doubt all along, roared away, there was a noise in his ears of his own blood. They *would* meet again! They had to go on! He wanted Beatrix more than he wanted to live. Finally astonished, he heard himself say that and heard that was true.

Beatrix let herself into the house and stood in the hall calling 'Simon?' quietly so as not to wake the children. He was not yet back and she hung up her coat, before going upstairs to look in on them.

Sam was four and Cleo was two. Sam lay on his back, his fists either side of his face, entrusted to sleep. Only the top of Cleo's head showed from a carefully constructed nest of bedclothes. They were different in the way they slept. Two people.

Often when Beatrix had left Colm it had been because she wanted to see them, or because it was the time they expected to see her. She'd never come back to them from a sense of duty. In fact, she was amazed how little conflict there was between her feeling for Colm and what it implied. Sam and Cleo were people themselves and she felt no need to protect their innocence by over-examining her own. They were not entrenchments to hide behind, responsibilities to remember. She could not imagine forgetting them. It had made her sad sometimes, the thought of the possible disruption in all their lives, but there seemed no question of not doing something 'for the sake of the children'. They were as much a part of her as her limbs. They were more important to her than they were to Simon, he'd admit it. He liked playing with them, was fond of them, but soon bored. As to what would happen – this was not the time to think of it. Whatever it was she wouldn't allow it to affect them badly because if she protected herself she would protect them, it was the same thing, If she tried to think any other way she floundered in other peoples' maxims and rules that had no meaning for her at this time.

There were clues she had to follow. If she'd discovered one false note she would have stopped. But she hadn't.

She went downstairs to wait for Simon.

She sat in her own chair, her island in Simon's room, cushioned, covered in soft red tweed, she always slid off Simon's leather furniture. They didn't sit here together often nowadays. It wasn't that they'd drawn apart – if anything they were closer, she less of the dazzled schoolgirl, Simon more of an equal – but he was so busy these times, dashing about. Perhaps he'd always been like that – it was true her growing-up had taken a different pace, had become quieter. A little, she thought, they'd become like brother and sister; incestuous, but it was their friendship that was strongest. She didn't think that was second-best, she didn't measure it at all. She and Simon were two, together, married, parents, old friends; they loved each other. As she'd written in the notebook (how unhelpful *that* had turned out to be), he knew her and she knew him.

She had a moment of sickness. She heard the door, and Simon came into the hall. She wasn't ready, she was drowning, these waters moved too fast. She felt like Maggie Tulliver in the flood, the world was changed and ugly, doom-filled.

Simon came in. 'Hi,' he said and touched the back of her head, going to pour himself a drink at the corner table.

It often took her by surprise how beautiful he was. His hair fitted his scalp like a marvellous cap – she felt the original Adam's hair must have been like that, it looked as natural as fur, or the forehead locks of a slender, pacific bull. His shirt collar always showed above his jacket, higher than anybody else's (although some of the young boys nowadays were doing the same thing). This gave him his eighteenth-century look, nineteenth, timeless really. She loved the way he had always known so surely his own style. And she loved his eyes, almost black, in his pale, triangular face; never judging; filled with a kind of inextinguishable faith in pleasure. Now he came to sit opposite her with his drink of lime juice and ice, they'd probably made him drink more than he wanted to after his show. He drew up his knees on the long sofa-thing with the nude men at either end. What a ridiculous piece of furniture that was!

'It went rather well,' he said cheerfully. She'd forgotten to ask him! There'd been a preview of his film about dockside pubs. It was difficult to take an interest in Simon's work because he always treated it as a joke himself, but she should have asked him – he'd been worried about it.

'What have you been doing?'

'Oh, I went out to dinner with a chum.' She'd been going out a good deal lately, but he'd never asked her further. What did Simon think she did? When she'd left Colm she had known what she had to do. But how could she?

'Simon. I've got something to tell you.'

'Oo!'

He always made fun of her when she was serious. She liked it – there were occasions when he turned to her, serious himself, vulnerable, and she made fun of him, cheering him up. It seemed to work out fifty-fifty. She'd read novels, mostly by women, in which this 'There, there' habit of men was regarded as hateful. She'd never been able to see why, or think of it as particularly male. There were so many balances and counterweights between two people that didn't matter a bit if they liked each other. She liked Simon very much.

'Oh, Simon darling, I think I've fallen for somebody else.'

He gasped with laughter. 'Bea! You sly old thing! So *that's* what you've been up to!'

She nodded. She'd done it. Let it take its course.

He looked at her, still smiling, watching her face. He put his drink down on the floor.

'I hadn't thought of that. Is it serious?'

She couldn't answer.

'Crumbs!' He got up and stood at the fireplace, his arms on the huge mantel. She remembered when they'd found that, Simon's shouts of pleasure when he'd seen it. He rested his face between his arms and stared down at the electric fire. 'Actually that's not true. I *have* thought of it. Of course. You're so marvellous and good – how could somebody else not notice? Bea,' he turned to her and squatted in front of her, taking both her hands, 'you are all that, you know, and more. It's so marvellous with you – everything – that's not over, is it? No,' he said, getting up, gathering his glass, going to the corner and pouring a proper drink, 'Of course it isn't.'

'Could I have one?' This was bad in a different way to the one she'd expected – unreal. She couldn't be having this conversation with Simon.

'What's his name? Anyone I know?'

'Colm Treacey.'

He stood, holding the two glasses, looking at her. She wondered what Simon made of Colm. He gave no sign.

'What do you want to do?'

She wanted to say 'I don't know', put it all on to him. 'He wants me to go on a holiday with him. Two weeks.'

'And you'd like to?'

She nodded.

He handed her the drink. 'You must go. Of course.' Then he knelt in front of her.

'I can't bear to see you looking so miserable.' He gave a small laugh. 'It's all right. Really it is. I've never known you do a thing that didn't seem to me exactly right. I've never told you that, have I? Other people have a way of taking detours,' he made streaking motions with his hand, 'you have a way of going straight there – bang. So if you want to do this it must be right.' He began to grin. 'But I'm not going to let you go as easily as that! I can't very well grab a horse-whip, though, can I?'

She had been able to start this scene – just – but since then she had felt drained of everything except a desire for sleep. Simon was still smiling, but there was strain in it, he was keeping the smile on his face which was something she had never seen him do. Then he said, 'Have you...?

She knew what he meant and shook her head.

'... I'm so glad. Silly, isn't it! So unjustified.... Well – I've got you tonight haven't I? Let's go to bed.'

'Oh, let's!'

'You *are* a shameless woman!'

She giggled, exhausted. He helped her from the chair. They stood, his arm round her, her head on his shoulder and that way they walked to the door.

'I feel like a seducer,' he said.

Suddenly she kissed him in a way they hadn't kissed for a long time. After it they were moved, embarrassed as strangers. Still in the same position, her head on his shoulder, her feet dragging, they went upstairs to their room.

In the morning Simon seemed very cheerful, as though the new quantity in our lives was giving him an extra charge of excitement. His mood affected me. Maybe our lives were at stake, but why so solemn? In fact, after half an hour of Simon dashing up and down stairs, winking at me through the bedroom door –

wagging his finger, cursing as he rummaged – he could never find what he had to take with him in the mornings – and then out through the front door his overcoat billowing behind him, calling out 'Be good!' and laughing, I began to wonder if it wasn't the only way to deal with such things, to turn them into a game. Perhaps the serious things are too much for us to take seriously – we have to let them take us.

Feeling very strange, as though coming round from an anaesthetic, I telephoned Colm at his office. He sounded strange too, straining to hear things in my voice but I didn't care what he heard or know what there was to hear. I didn't feel anything except blindfolded, moving from one landmark to another that I would only recognize when I reached it. He suggested we meet at a restaurant in Charlotte Street, which was strange because I knew it was the sort of place he hated.

I got there before he did and was shown to a table by a discreet Greek: snowy tablecloths, silvery silver, noiseless trolleys, and at every table assured-looking people murmuring to each other. Then Colm appeared, stood inside the door looking for me. For the first time I saw him in a dark suit, his hair brushed, his cuffs as white as the tablecloths and I saw why he had arranged for us to meet here. He'd decided to draw a circle round this meeting. This was no-man's-land, stagey setting for the Start of an Affair, a moment we were past and therefore safe from. Here, the smart table between us, Colm in his best suit looking like a dissipated 1940s film actor, the ridiculousness, the barbarousness even, of the little scene we had to play was heightened nearly out of existence. This was a true instinct of his because the situation was dangerously absurd. I couldn't behave like a conspirator – 'So I said to Simon and he said to me' – whispering over the wineglasses. There was little I could say, Colm would have to guess.

He sat down opposite me, smiling carefully. The waiter hovered and he ordered for us both, I doubt if he knew what. Not knowing where to begin, he began about himself.

'I felt I'd deserted you at the foot of the scaffold.'

'It was a bit like that. . . . What did you do?'

'Strode off into the night blaspheming. Drank some brandy.'

'I told Simon.'

He stared away from me across the room, his face silhouetted against the dark red hangings on the far wall.

'It's all done,' I said.

'Did he . . .'

'Simon's very marvellous.' I said it as gently as I could, but it wasn't my job to reassure him about Simon. I knew that if we discussed him, ganged up against him, things would start to go wrong. Simon was my business.

'When shall we go?' said Colm.

'Any time you like.'

He let out a little slow escape of breath as though he'd been holding his lungs full. 'Today's Friday. Sunday?'

'All right.'

'Wow!' he said, looking at the tablecloth.

'Where shall we go?'

'Well, I've been thinking. I've a friend who'd lend us a cottage on the West Coast of Ireland . . .' his voice trailed away, he was watching me.

A lonely cottage, wind, rain and sea and us looking at each other, a little frightened, like a Victorian honeymoon.

He went on. 'I'm not sure that isn't a bit self-conscious. . . . I tried to think of somewhere easy – sun and bars and so on – where we could just be together without having to work at it. I thought of one place – you'll probably laugh. Maybe you've been there already?' He looked glum suddenly.

'Where?'

'That place they're always writing about in the papers. Saint Donate.'

'Oh yes!'

'*Have* you been there?'

'No. I believe it's lovely.'

'Not too spoilt?'

'Hopelessly I expect. That's what's nice.'

He laughed with relief. I think he'd really feared I might sneer – had a vision of my 'circle' laughing at the mention of such a place. He didn't know me well if he thought that, but this was not an easy occasion; there were plenty of mistakes waiting to be made. I made one myself. When the bill came I guessed it would be big so I took roughly half from my handbag, scrunched it up in my fist and pushed my closed hand across the table.

'What's that?'

'Do take it. The bill must be vast.'

'Oh, money.... Why have you crumpled it like that?' The waiter was standing near, Colm made sure he heard. 'Thank you – yes – very useful.' He carefully smoothed out the notes, added some of his own, and the waiter swept them up.

'Wow!' said Colm again, about the bill.

'And I'm going to pay half of the holiday.' The waiter arrived with the change, Colm stared down at it calculating the tip, said 'Whoopee!' in answer to me, absentmindedly, but he had heard and he had agreed. He pushed the plate with some coins on it aside and handed me two half-crowns.

'We've got a lot to talk about.'

'It can wait for a bit, can't it?'

'Yes, it can wait.' He put his hand over mine suddenly. 'We won't let anything unnecessary spoil it, will we? Some things are unavoidable. We won't let anything we *can* avoid spoil it?' He was inviting my carefulness as well as his own. 'Let's go slow.'

'Oh yes – let's go slow!'

This was our moment of greatest closeness so far, absurd and true – not telling each other how much we loved and so on, but here in this crowded expense-account restaurant counselling each other to be careful. It was a childish joy to me that so much was so different from all I'd been told. It was like a guarantee that we were on the right track, not inventing. If he'd swept me off my feet, shown me a new world, king-like, with one of those expansive map-unrolling gestures that some men are fond of, I'd have been forced to play the beggar-maid, wrapped in my pretended admiration like a false fur. As it was we were both the same size, small and surprised. This was how I'd always wanted it to be: the smallness of me, the largeness of it, and the chance of both of us growing.

We stood on the pavement outside the restaurant as the cars snicked past and the sun caught the top windows of the houses. It was very cold, the sky a thin parting in a head of houses and we were both big with overcoats and scarves. Colm's nostrils had gone red at the wings and his eyes were watering. I felt mine water too.

'You look beautiful,' he said, and brushed my cheek with his; it was warm, almost burning. Our faces were the only naked part of us, the rest was in layers of cloth thick as armour, we were two parcels in the wind.

'Would you rather fly or go by train?'

'Train.' Slow. Slower the better.

'O.K. I'll ring you the time. I can't see you till then.'

We'd reached a point. The next one was Sunday.

He stopped a taxi and I got in. 'When shall I ring you?' he said, not wanting to get Simon.

'Lunchtime tomorrow.' He stood back and the taxi pulled away. I wanted to call out – No, not Sunday, let's meet tonight, Sunday's too far away – I was too slow, the taxi moved on and I looked at Colm through the back window standing on the pavement in his overcoat, his hair lifting awkwardly in the wind, a cold man on a street corner watching a taxi until it disappeared.

To scurry back to Simon and tell him the travelling arrangements was grotesque, but he had to be told. Salutary the way the absurd kept breaking in – clicking the mind away from the wrong kind of intensity – the big world outside still turned, unshaken.

Simon was taking the whole thing so well by now that he might have been heaping coals of fire, but he didn't mean to.

'Sunday morning on the Blue Train? How *louche*! I think I'd better move into my dressing-room, don't you? That's what one does, I think. No – it's usually her that insists.' He imitated Margaret Dumont and Groucho. 'Hubert – you'll sleep in your dressing-room tonight.' 'I insist on sleeping in my pajamas!' The fact that Simon's dressing-room was a lumber-room much blitzed by Sam and Cleo did not deter him, he relished the drama of it. Out all Friday until late, he came back a little drunk and tiptoed cheerfully through their bedroom trying not to wake Beatrix, making shushing noises to himself. She heard him, but said nothing because she could think of nothing to say. There were no sheets on the camp-bed in that little room. She hadn't felt able to prepare a bed for him in there – it seemed so odd – but in the end she couldn't bear it, put on the light, fetched some sheets from the landing and took them in to him.

'Do get up – you can't possibly sleep in those filthy old blankets.'

'What? Oh. You interrupted me. I was imagining myself one of the Desert Fathers. D'you know they used to compete who could get the most lice in his beard?'

He got up obediently and stood long-legged in his black pyjamas playing with Sam's fire-engine on the table-top while she made his bed.

'There you are.'

'You are sweet. No I shall pretend to be Lord Nelson.'

The tiny bed did look rather bunk-like. He inserted himself carefully so as not to disturb her tuckings-in. 'You do make a good bed, Bea, I must say.'

'Shall I put the light out?'

'Yes do. Nelson at what stage d'you think? Before he met Emma Hamilton or after?'

As she got back into bed she heard him murmur, 'Perhaps it would be more appropriate to be Sir William?'

Part of Simon's attitude derived from a simple wish not to complicate things, but he was also genuinely puzzled. How could he blame Beatrix, or complain, when he could imagine himself behaving in the same way? It was perfectly on the cards that he might fall in love as (presumably) she had done and he always reserved himself the right, and granted her the same, to pursue the matter as far as need be. Of course. And yet he was frightened. In his own phrase he preferred to twitter among the topmost branches of his life, thinking about its roots as little as possible but now these were working loose. He needed Beatrix. He supposed he loved her. Doubtless, if the worst happened, he could learn in time to do without her. But the superficiality of his life had always seemed to him a chosen attitude, founded on strong untalked-about things underneath. (How God-awful that sounded!) Beatrix was the most important of those things. If she'd had enough of him who *was* he for heaven's sake? The droll fellow he looked like from outside?

If she wanted to go he couldn't stop her. Should he make a scene, show how much he cared? Perhaps even Beatrix might want that. Was she shocked by all this revolting good behaviour? Judging her by himself, which he always did, he imagined she was confused by this new thing, wanting to find out about it before coping with any decision. So he let her be, hoping he was right.

He was helped by being very busy. The whole of Saturday he spent at the television studios and that night he appeared as a guest on the late show; he loved that, the excitement and the showing off, knew he was good at it. Coming back very late he crept past their bed with Beatrix in it – asleep he hoped, awake he also hoped, about to call him. However she was indeed asleep and he went again to the camp-bed; she had made it up for him.

In the morning he heard her moving about early, a taxi whirring outside. He didn't call to her. Then he heard the front door slam. Silence. Then the taxi door slammed and it revved away. After a second or two of blankness he jumped up and stuck his head out of the window. Silly thing to do. The street was empty, of course.

Quite soon Sam and Cleo erupted into his room. Later the papers arrived and he discovered, as he'd half-suspected, that he'd been a great success the previous night; 'TV NATURAL' was one headline, and other papers went on about him too. In fact, he had been in tremendous form, had rattled away, unable to stop. Not that he'd been hiding a broken heart – he didn't feel it was broken.

Later in the day, Sam and Cleo resting, the telephone having stopped ringing, he found himself in their bedroom, looking at their bed, only a half of it rumpled, the impression of Beatrix's body still there. Oh, Bea, don't go! he heard himself say: Don't go! He saw he was holding one of her things, her nightdress, soft and thin and light-coloured, he put it over the brass bed-rail where it hung limp and still. He couldn't think how else he had expected it to hang, but its noiseless obedience suddenly appalled him. He flicked at one of the brass balls at the bed-foot, it didn't ring, gave a dull phut noise and hurt his nail. The objects in the room were heavy, waiting for him to give them back their life, waiting, if necessary, for ever. It occurred to him, for the first time, that *things* outlasted one, were in fact waiting for one to die. Somewhere in the house a cistern gave a soft gurgling sigh. Outside there was the occasional hissing swish of a rare Sunday car. He fled.

Technically it was Ita's, the au pair girl's, day off, but presumably Beatrix had explained to her, she showed no signs of going out. In fact her various thoughtful silences all over the house were among the worst things. He decided to go out himself. He rang up Thin, a tubular photographers' model who was at that time very smart indeed for reasons that were obscure to him and probably to everyone else. Thin was, in fact, her name, and at one time she had tried to spell it Thynne but a cute PR man had soon stopped that. Now there were Thin hair-cuts and Thin eye make-ups and, for all he knew, Thin-jokes. He'd take her to Decibelle's or The Electric Prune and enjoy watching the heads swivel. He might even talk to her if you could talk to that inviolable absence of response. At least she moved, unlike everything in the house except the hands of the clock.

He was mildly surprised at his lack of friends. He would have liked to talk to someone. In fact, ardent believer in friendliness though he was, he didn't believe in friendships of a heart-to-heart nature. It never seemed quite to work and if it did was a substitute for something else. Friendships were based on mutual interests, comradeships, and these changed with time, anything else savoured of Reunion, those ghastly cerebrations of a capitalized Past or – even worse, of Confidants – I say old chap my marriage is a bit rocky! – My dear old boy! Come in and sit down! ... Those who talked of having Friends usually meant a Gang inside which they went on tasting themselves and into which they burrowed, like a piece of old cheese.

However, movement was required. The town had created from its own emptiness its own values and he would have thought it absurd to live in the town and stay outside these sulking. All that dashing about, all those gestures, cut the air and burned it, their friction produced a form of light existing only in the town and (obviously, it seemed to Simon) he wished it also to shine on him. He played the town's game and would have thought it hopelessly arrogant, even masturbatory, to refuse.

At least from Thin he would be able to gauge his smartness-count after last night. For such matters, and for no others at all, Thin had the sensitivity of a medium. How marvellous of the journalists to think that the 'new' London of The Beautiful People because it had a cockney accent was therefore unsnobbish! Girls like Thin were the Lady Troubridges *de nos jours*. Not a nuance of in-ness escaped her while all the time she looked as though it cost her too many calories to breathe. As he dialled her number he sighed for the days when success could be measured by the affability of the Prince of Wales' nod. Simple, innocent folk! Now the tides and undertows were indicated by trance-state Sybils like Thin whose balance the smallest breath of humour, even of thought, would destroy. There was no reply. She was probably asleep, her connection switched off. A thought struck him: how did she distinguish sleep from that normal waking state?

He put on his overcoat in the hall intending to go for a walk and was then paralysed by the thought of the Sunday afternoon Boltons; householders with plastic buckets washing cars. Still in his overcoat, he went back to the drawing-room and switched on the television; quickly switched it off again. His only hope was that that Treacey chap was as withdrawn as he remembered him looking. She'd be halfway across France by now. He tried Thin again and her toneless Edgware voice faintly reached his ear. 'This is a recorded announcement. Please leave your name and number.' 'Thin, you little tart!' he shouted. 'It's me, Simon!' 'Hi love,' she said, her voice unchanged. She was meeting Rheingold at The Amusement Parlour. He hated that place with its illuminated wall-tanks of piranha fish swimming among (he hoped) plastic skeletons that reminded him of Thin. But he had liked Rheingold ever since he'd mentally dressed him in a burnoose and seen that amiably guileful countenance correctly framed, even dignified. Something would be sure to brew up there. He arranged to join them. Meanwhile there was the rest of the grisly afternoon to cope with and Simon discovered that what he most wanted to do was sleep. As soon as he admitted this to himself he had the greatest difficulty remaining upright. He pulled himself to the long sofa, cradled his head on the small of the back of one of the lovingly moulded end-pieces (the other would have been too spiky) and no sooner had he stretched himself out, still in his overcoat, than he ceased to hear the silence of the house, or the silence outside; all his objects stood patiently round, watching, waiting for Simon to wake (or die), but for the moment invisible to everyone, except, presumably, God.

8

The Blue Train clacked through green France, a brown tube, checking speed at grey obstructions which were towns, these becoming more yellow, more red, as they journeyed south.

Colm had booked a Pullman – this seemed no occasion to share the night with others – and they sat amid faded Edwardian splendours (also brown) awaiting curtain-up. Colm had nearly bought a box of chocolates at the station so much did the decorations of their compartment remind them both of a theatre.

The dinner in the restaurant-car was splendid; seven courses plonked in front of them by swaying, sweating waiters, each course more delicious than the last. Only the wine was a disappointment, tasted odd. Colm worked his way through the bottle, nevertheless, Beatrix drinking very little. Towards the end of the meal, frowning over his glass, still wondering, but content, a Frenchman on the other side of the car asked him what was the matter. The wine? Allow me to taste.... Corked! His decision was instant and indignant. There was a summoning of waiters, sippings, swillings, suckings-in of cheeks. Another bottle was brought, to Colm's dismay, he had already had more than enough. Beatrix wouldn't help, found the whole thing, Colm's hopeless entanglement in what looked now like a drinking competition, very funny, and left them to it, went back to their compartment. Colm insisted the Frenchman share the new bottle with him – he was now going off about les bons vins de France. That bottle finished, his antagonist insisted they share *his* nearly untouched bottle in the emptying dining-car. Colm, glassy-eyed, could think of no way to escape. They toasted each other frequently: the Frenchman saying 'Vive la France!' to which the only reply at this stage seemed 'Vive l'Angleterre!' He told Colm how happy he must be to have left poor foggy, bankrupt England, to be now in la Belle France – have some more bon vin! Have cognac! No thanks. It arrived, nevertheless. He bought one back: the process was repeated. No reason why it should ever stop unless the bill came, which it did and was enormous. Colm had to change some pounds to save currency for their journey onwards. The exchange-rate seemed lethal. He was watched pityingly by his companion as he attempted to do sums in his fuddle. The money-haemorrhage, always worse in France than anywhere else, had begun. Never mind. He was happy, in spite of this dreadful man with whom he seemed to be spending the night. The Frenchman had now reached the morose stage. Colm stood up and patted him on his bald head, 'Vive les bons vins de France!' he said amiably. The other belched. 'Vive le déficit Anglais!' 'Vive la Manche!' riposted Colm, delighted with himself, and they shook hands formally, the Frenchman half-rising, subsiding again with a soft pouf! as he encountered the edge of the table.

Leaving him, Colm found the corridor full of unpredictable angles. A particularly sharp collision made him pause long enough to realize what he'd done: the perfectly inappropriate thing; he'd got hopelessly, incapably drunk. He was also drunk enough to find it fairly funny. Start as you mean to go on, etc. Perhaps he'd half-consciously intended this? There was a part of him that was scared stiff. Never mind, there were other parts – not tonight there weren't ho! ho! Bang! (Perhaps this train kept on turning corners?) Things weren't going according to plan. Or rather, in the absence of a plan, they weren't going according to dream. So much the better. The ludicrous seemed to him a strengthening factor, like the stones they put in cement. Why be rude about dreams? Being awake is never half as real as a dream while you're dreaming it. He stuck his head out of the window and through watering eyes noted with approval that Orion kept his station, that Castor and Pollux guarded left and right, insisting on the middle way. He decided to follow their example for the rest of his progress down the train.

Beatrix was in her bunk.

At once he was sober, for a moment at least, and on his knees beside her. He buried his face in the pillow next to hers, putting his arm round her warmth under the bed clothes. He raised his head and looked at her face, then he looked at his own bunk. This was their moment. Whose? It was the train's, the night's, the Frenchman's, not theirs. He'd spent his life cheerfully putting up with the second-best. Not this time. He jumped up quickly, took off some clothes and climbed down between the sheets of his bunk. He reached across for her hand. She had her eyes closed now, turned a little away, seemed content. This was his last chance. If he'd been misled, waiting gormlessly for the right music and had thereby lost her, he'd never listen for it again, he'd use his common sense for Christ's sake, he'd be a man, my son! Her hand went slack and he disengaged their fingers. She was asleep. The mud at the bottom of his mind had been stirred as though with a stick; lighting a cigarette, he waited for it to settle, comforted by the little red glow in the dark. He opened the window, the noise of the train doubled but she didn't stir. She was here. She was with him. The inside of his head stayed cloudy, whirling, that piece of knowledge was all he had. They were together. The words stayed with him, turning round, 'they were together', mingled with the clacking of the wheels.

Next morning, very early, they sat drinking coffee in the bar outside Saint Raphael station waiting for the bus that would take them on. It was cold at that hour in early May and Beatrix was muffled in her coat like a blanket, warming her face in the steam of her coffee.

'Your coat's the colour of dried rose leaves in a bowl,' he said (because it was). 'And your face comes out of the top like an ice-cream.'

'It feels like an ice-cream.'

He put his nose near her cheek, bending over. 'Warm bedclothes and biscuits,' he said. 'You look Chinese when you've just woken up.'

She studied him over the top of her cup of coffee, holding it with both hands. 'Your hair's standing on end.'

Quickly he tried to tamp it down with his hands. 'Better?'

It wasn't, but she nodded, laughing. He was unshaven, slowed down by the unaccustomed early-rising, hung-over, a little sheepish.

'More coffee?' He went to the bar and ordered it with a Fernet Branca for himself, enjoying asking for a drink at 7.30 in the morning, also needing it. He drained the glass and made a face. 'Ugh! That man last night! Good God!' he'd seen himself in the mirror behind the bar, 'why didn't you tell me?'

'I thought you'd rather not know.'

He brought the coffee over and stood. 'Have I told you how beautiful you look?'

'No.'

He sat down opposite her and she put her hand over his, feeling him go still, as though measuring the exact weight of it.

'Where's that bus?' He pushed his chair back, yawning, waving his clenched fist across his mouth as though to drive the yawn away, but it got wider. 'Pooh!' he shook his head, 'I feel exhausted after that night's rest. Another Fernet Branca perhaps...?'

'You dare!'

'Quite.'

The bus came and took them towards the coast and then along it. Fringed with tiny brand-new villas and scarred sites for newer ones. The morning sea was very calm, like a lake, and near the shore had bits of rubbish floating in it, barely moving, white and blue polythene containers for washing-up liquid, bits of paper.

The bus station was a large square of asphalt like a parade ground, surrounded by unfinished apartment buildings, newly glazed, with warning blobs of white distemper on their windows. The few other passengers on the bus gathered their parcels and vanished at once, so did the driver. They were alone in two acres of tarmac. Colm picked up their bags and they set off in what they hoped was the direction of the sea. Eventually, clambering over more building sites, and then more, they reached a view of the harbour, much be-yachted, shiny with rows of sportive cars.

Colm put down the bags and stared. Then he looked at her and picked up the bags again.

At last they found someone, an old man sitting on a box, a genuine inhabitant by the look of his teak face and the shortness of his pipe. He knew the hotel Colm had been told about in London. He gave them directions. It was the far side of the town.

Taking turns with the bags (it was a long way) they walked slowly round the harbour, past an old tower, into a good white-washed square with boutiques and hairdressers and jazzy *crêpes* shops in it, but also with little grocers, warty old women in black already sitting outside them with boxes of tomatoes the size of cooking-apples, absorbed in pieces of knitting, also black. They bent further over their knitting, silent, as Colm and Beatrix passed. Then, under an old cracked arch with a tree growing out of the top, round a corner, behind another tree, was the hotel he'd heard of in the old port, with fishing-nets spread over the wall to dry, tiny silver fish still caught in some of the tangles. Would there be room? (There were anxieties in this careful cultivation of chance.) The proprietor was found – snub-nosed, like Socrates with a burned-out yellow cigarette dangling from his lip. He took his time, looking them over. Did he have a room? Perhaps. Passports? Colm had forgotten that. Different names. Perhaps they refused adulterers in France? Socrates muttered something through his cigarette and a girl appeared, led them up the cool shuttered stairs.

The room was dark, large, floored with blue tiles that had a thick translucent glaze on them, it was like walking on the sea. He gave the girl some money, she went away and he locked the door. Then he went to the window and opened the shutters. The sun, well up now, the last morning mist had gone, crashed into the room and the sea was under the window. Beatrix let her coat fall on to the large white bed and her yellow linen dress caught the sun, her arms, bare to above the shoulder, hanging at her sides. She stood, yellow and white against the shining blue of the floor. He pushed the shutters ajar again, so that there was only a glow in the room, full of shadows, and the soft sucking noise of the water outside.

He went towards her. The last weeks, the journey last night, the barely suppressed anxieties of the last hour, gathered and burst in a soft tide. There was no fumbling, neither of them could remember any. It had the inevitability they had waited for.

After a while they heard the first mid-morning swifts begin their screeching, come close to the window, casting their quick shadows.

'The Angel of the Vision,' he murmured. 'What happened?'

Her head was on his arm, heavy as a baby's. Without moving his arm he pulled his own head away to look at her. Her eyes were half-closed. She raised her lids as though drawing up a heavy curtain. She shook her head.

'Why can't we say? Why do all the best things have to be dumb? Why can't we prove things to people who don't believe them?' His voice was strange. 'I've never known anything like it.'

'No.'

They turned towards each other again, their eyes open as though moving towards each other now across a cleared space, keeping themselves conscious, hardly daring to believe. She felt as if her life had become a series of sliding platforms, each one uncovering another below. There was more to happen yet, further to go. It had to go on, this process of sliding away, and sensed in him the same awed determination. The last of the platforms was going, it wasn't only physical, it was revealing a part of herself that she didn't know, that now belonged to him as well and some part of him was being revealed that she could never lose. It was simple – there were colours – white and blue and yellow.

'I didn't know!' she cried.

'Neither did I.'

Afterwards, after a long silence, Colm became gay, even offhand. While they dressed to go out and find some lunch, standing at the window he'd murmured to himself: 'It's a helluva song and dance to make.' The tone of it stopped her impatience. It was a quotation from another Colm and she heard the wonder in his voice as he found that he no longer knew what that self was talking about. The defences he put up between himself and the possibly false or exaggerated were an extreme of concentration that made her feel safe. He gave the impression that where he finally chose to stand would be entirely solid.

They had lunch at one of the restaurants on the port, almost the only people in it, the season had not yet started. In spite of the sun it was still cold. They sat outside to begin with but were soon driven in by the nagging wind. They both drank too much wine.

'Perhaps they're right to make a religion out of sex.'

'Who?'

'Haven't you heard? Fifty per cent say Whoopee! Fifty per cent say Disgusting! One hundred per cent Don't know.... If that isn't a religion I don't know what is.'

'Which side are you on?'

'Neither, worse luck.'

'Why worse luck?'

'You have to be a very good musician to be pig in the middle. It's easier to knock things down.'

'Oh – !'

'Knocking down bad old things is good. But there isn't much left. Now it's a question of rebuilding properly an old, razed ground. That can look like reaction, or nostalgia.'

'Does it matter what it looks like?'

'Very much. If it sounds the wrong sort of harking-back no one will listen – or only the wrong ones.

'I wrote a piece in College once – straight from the heart, so I thought. I was taken up by a big-wig, given a prize. I was delighted until I realized he'd only liked the piece because it was unlike all the contemporaries I admired. He thought it was like Brahms.'

'What did you do with the prize?'

'Spent it.'

'Would it ever be possible to say what happened this morning "straight out"?'

'If I could I'd be a great composer. If I tried and failed –'

'You'd be given a knighthood.'

'... It *was* mysterious, wasn't it.'

'Well ... no. That's the funny thing. I didn't feel it was. I saw – colours....'

'How d'you mean?'

'Everything in white and gold and blue. Not golden gold. Strong yellow. People, I mean. Houses. Clear cut – not at all mysterious. As though I'd always seen things like that, only I'd forgotten.'

'Changed?' He'd put down his knife and fork.

'No. Not. Just themselves. Me, beds, windows, trains. Everything. It was as if . . .'

'As if what?'

'It was like being reminded that there is a *soft* surface to the world as well. No,' she hurried on, 'soft's not the right word. Not mushy or crumbly or weak in any way but bright and strong and – *sweet.*' She thought he might interrupt her, but he didn't. 'I mean – we try and face up to the horribleness. We have to do that. Perhaps we have to face up to the other as well. It seemed – to be waiting for us.'

Colm was silent. Then he waved his knife in the direction of the port. 'Pirates. Everyone happy enough fishing, little houses, white gold and blue; and then – nothing – blood, flames.'

'But Colm I *know*! So we become pirates ourselves – to defend ourselves. A bit of our nature gets lost. It's like – refusing to enjoy a tree because one day somebody'll chop it down. It takes *courage* to expose ourselves to the soft part of the world!'

To her astonishment he was blushing, staring at her, his eyes wide.

He busied himself with his plate. 'Where were we?'

'Sex.'

'It *must* be getting late! Are the waiters looking impatient?' He turned to see. They were taking the tablecloths from the surrounding tables. 'The tide's coming in,' he said, happily, filling both their glasses from the last of the bottle, and began to talk fast, excitedly.

'We live in a tent, I think. We push at it with our minds and it bags a little, the tent-space gets that much bigger, but it's still a tent and we're still inside. But what about the times like this morning when the flaps and toggles are easy, we stick our heads right out. It's fantastic! Look! We pull our heads back in to tell the others, but it closes behind us and they won't believe us. We begin to doubt it ourselves. How do those moments come, though? And what can we do while we're waiting for them to come back?'

'That's what religions are for, I suppose.'

'Christianity's the best of all religions,' he startled her by saying. 'The only feasible approach to suffering. The trouble is we're a practical lot, we Western Europeans. Hanging round waiting can look a bit woolly so our religion busies itself with tent-organization instead of keeping an eye on the flap. The end-result is a parade of nuns with banners: "Bomb Hanoi".'

They stood up to leave. "I'm drunk,' he said. 'Talking too much.'

'There's plenty of time, Colm. The rest of our lives.' He stopped and stared ahead and she went on. 'This morning happened to me too, you know. But it wasn't that. I'd known all along, I think.'

He stared and then he pulled his hand down over his nose and mouth, pulling them out of shape, shook his head as though trying to shake away cobwebs. Then he looked at her and laughed and she took his arm.

They went out into the sun and were blinded by it. A sleepy afternoon had settled on the harbour and on the town they walked through on the way back to their hotel.

In the days that followed it seemed to Beatrix that Colm was in the grip of an excitement that made him talk like a boy, laying himself open for inspection. She was startled by the starkness of some of the things she saw in him, but when he sensed this he put them away, he set great store by ordinary happiness, regarding it as a special form of insight. He still flailed around, prodding, pushing, sometimes tripping them both with the violence of his shadow-boxing, but it was this that made Beatrix feel her need for him. Her sureness would have been useless, inert, without his extravagant suspicion. Although she knew she helped him, helped them both, these words 'need', 'help', were not the right ones, were near-misses to the truth and therefore dangerous. Their life together wasn't a series of physical contacts followed by warm voids, they continued to touch each other all the time, through talk and through silence. She encouraged him to do most of the talking because it made the right sound in both their ears, she was the auditorium in which he played out one side of their life for both of them. This wasn't a superior feeling, without him the theatre would have been empty, and without the theatre, his voice, which was both their voices, would have been lost on the air.

They found a small beach near their hotel. It was reached by a narrow path along a rocky hillside and just before it was a walled enclosure jutting into the sea; the town cemetery. They exclaimed when they first saw it because of the colours of the flowers on every grave, but when they got near and leaned over the wall they saw that all the wreaths, even the tiny brilliantly coloured posies of wild flowers in jars filled with water, were made of porcelain.

'The thrifty French,' said Colm, and fell silent. Then he told her of a friend of his who had died, making the word 'death' real to him, till then it had just been a sound. Beatrix was quiet in her turn, unable to think about it but he insisted, said we had to think of it to be more aware of what was still alive, real mortal flowers, not china ones. He dragged her into the water (it was their first swim and the water was not warm) made her swim out farther than she wanted and hugged her there out of their depth, both of them rolling over and over, tasting salt because their mouths kept opening to laugh. But he was fascinated by those wreaths and stopped to stare at them every time they passed.

One morning when they were lying on the sand he said: 'I don't think the world's a tent after all. If so, it's such a big one it doesn't count. Plotinus says our treasures are inside us – we have to go diving for them. Maybe that's true.' He raised himself on his elbow and peered down at her. 'Then of course there's Leibnitz. What are your views on Leibnitz?'

Beatrix groaned, a straw hat tilted over her eyes.

'Interesting you should say that.... He was of the opinion that we are composed of a number of unconnected particles, none of which is aware of what the others are up to – or cares for that matter. He called the particles monads and declared them windowless.' He groaned now, flicking sand over himself. 'Mind you,' he added thoughtfully, 'I've known *people* like that.'

He meant the two friends of Simon's they'd met the afternoon before in a bar on the port.

When they'd seen Beatrix they were of course fascinated by

what they'd stumbled across. Colm had been at his worst, drank far too much and then spent the rest of the time playing the pin-table machine at the other end of the bar.

'Who's the *friend?*' they whispered. She told them, furious with Colm for abandoning her like that. Also she noticed that in their striped blue T-shirts, blue denim trousers with bell-bottoms, and espadrilles, they made Colm look like something out of *Monsieur Hulot's Holiday* and irrationally she was furious with him for that too, although she hadn't noticed it before. They came from a yacht (which belonged to a friend of her mother's) and asked them both on board before dinner. She went to tell Colm, but he said 'You go', concentrated on waggling the flippers of the machine, muttering encouragement to the ball, watching the numbers ring up. So she did, angry.

On the yacht everything was as she'd expected. Pleasant enough, a life she had seen and never cared for. Everyone friendly in a self-absorbed way, long having known the little there was to know about each other, one or two quiet drunks, one or two tolerated spongers, gossip about acquaintances and the occupants of nearby villas. The two from the bar came over to her.

'He seems a bit of a bear your Mr T,' said one, as the other, a second-fiddle whom she had never liked, wound himself up for a coy rudeness.

'He appears to feel his platitudes contain the force of *Revelation!*'

That was true enough, Colm was obvious, he wanted to rediscover the simple in himself. He had no restlessness for novelty at all. And she had no business among these people any more.

She found him sitting at a table in a bar facing the port, writing music, something she'd never seen him do. He closed the notebook almost at once and then looked up, grinning. Beatrix saw there were four drink-slips on the table and a large glass of Pernod in front of him. 'Drink?' She shook her head.

'How was it?'

'Rotten. I wished you were there.'

'Thanks. How were Rosencrantz and Guildenstern?'

'Rosencrantz found you rather a dream and Guildenstern thought you went in for platitudes.'

He was taken aback, but rallied. 'Of course I do! I believe in gratitude for every platitude – grateful for my plateful.'

'What were you writing?'

'Us. Scored for two Euclids and a Rosencrantz. Did I tell you I was the reincarnation of Delius if I'm not careful? Plus mathematics. The whole wet wash of emotion explained like a theorem, Q.E.D., the balls go into the holes and the lights go on. Ping! No argument.'

'Shall we go for a walk?'

He stood up. 'I dreamed I was judged by a Bell-Bottomed Platypus – I mean Platitude. A curious creature, never seen to breed which nevertheless reproduces itself in each generation.' He giggled. 'Like money.' He began to sing to the tune of 'Oh dear what can the matter be'.

'I am a Bell-Bottomed Platitude.
When I bend over please fancy my attitude.
Do like this but don't like that-itude.
Let's have our bell-bottoms bare!'

'Colm. They don't matter.'

'I know *that*!' He laughed and put his arm round her shoulders, stiffly, keeping apart, not letting his side touch hers. They walked past the little stalls of holiday gear that stayed open late on the port. She stopped at one of these and picked up a blue cotton shirt, held it against him. He said nothing. She took a pair of pinkish trousers, held these against his side.

'I dress on the left.'

She bought both of them and they walked on.

'What does it feel like to be a gigolo?'

'I expect I shall have to work for it.'

'In that case I'll buy you some beach shoes.'

She carried the packages, he didn't offer to take them from her. They went on past the brightly lit section of the quay into the shadows away from the gramophones at the end where they could hear the water, look back at the lights shining on it, see the masts of the boats and the glow of the yacht she'd been on.

'Do you hate queers then?'

'Why on earth d'you ask that? ... Because of R. and G.? No, of course I don't. It's money I hate ... or fear, I suppose. It affects things. And people. Me no less than everyone else. I'm a man and men are meant to be Providers. I've barely managed to provide for myself so far and touch wood.'

'And now you have me?'

'Do I?'

'Yes.'

They stood looking across at the bright curve of the harbour, standing in the dark. 'There are problems. Money is one of them – don't say you have enough for us both or I'll push you in the harbour. Money's alive, a dozy animal, dangerous when poked – unless you're pure like a saint and I'm not. I think perhaps you are. But then you have it which makes it easier.'

'I know that.'

'I know you do. But don't you see, with your money my absurd job becomes even more absurd? Splendid! I can give it up and spend my life doing what I want to do. Then I become an amateur with music for a hobby.'

'Rubbish ...'

'Is it? How do I know what I'd be like when the pressure's off? I tell you money's alive like a third presence – it affects things between people – it might take years but it always gets its man.'

'Let's not talk about it now.'

'O.K.'

She imitated Guildenstern. 'I find your concern rather b-bourgeois.'

He laughed. 'Let's go somewhere I can afford for supper – restore my self-respect.' He took the packages she was holding. 'Thank you for my Rosenpants – they'll improve my Guildenstern.'

'For this thanks – much relief.'

'... Hey! That's *quick*!'

'I have my moments.'

They went to a little restaurant in the old town well away from the sea. It was cheap because the food was not very good, and empty for the same reason. But the mother and son who ran it were always so pleased to see them, so astonished probably, that it had become one of their most frequent places.

Beatrix told Colm about the man who owned the yacht, about her mother and her various step-fathers, official and otherwise. Then he began to talk about his own childhood for the first time. His father, an Irishman, had married an English waitress and died when Colm was a baby.

'Then my father's elder brother, who wouldn't have anything to do with him when he was alive – my father sounds rather splendid, a failed medical student, played the violin in some kind of scratch swing-band that was hired by hotels, that's how he met my mother – anyway this uncle was unmarried and didn't like the thought of his nephew not being a credit to him so he sort of took me over. I spent half my time in the big house in Cork and the other half with my mother.

'Uncle John didn't like children much. He left me to his housekeeper. When I arrived she threw away my clothes, put me in others more suitable, in her view, for a junior country-gent. When I went back to England my mother made me take them off. That happened every time.'

'Did your uncle send your mother money?'

'No. She wasn't accepted by the family.'

'Poor woman!'

'I was too young to take it all in, really. I preferred the house in Ireland on the whole – didn't like going back to the digs in London. My mother was always tired and I had to stay in the room while she was out working. She drank a bit.'

'What happened in the end?'

'When I was about ten they must have paid my mother off, or done something because I never lived with her after that. I went to a boarding school in England. In the holidays I either went to Ireland – learned to shoot with my cousins, riding, that sort of thing – or I stayed on at school. A few times I went to a holiday camp.'

'How awful!'

'No. I quite liked that. The holiday camp was pretty lousy but school was empty except for three or four of us, no rules to speak of, no work; I used to play the Headmaster's piano pretending I was Rachmaninov – much better than Ireland where all my cousins knew each other and I used to trail behind with the third-best gun thinking dark thoughts. Then I went to the College of Music – Uncle John gave me two thousand pounds and that's the last I heard from him. I won a prize which kept me going, stayed with friends or in digs, taught, did small commissions. – Here I am.'

'And your mother?'

'She died about ten years ago.'

'You never saw much of her?'

'Not really, no.'

'She must have hated giving you up.'

'I suppose so, yes. I saw her once, out shopping. We spoke, just chatted. It was odd.' He was silent for a moment, picking at crumbs on the tablecloth. 'If I had the time over again I'd behave differently to my mother.'

'What about the house in Ireland?'

'That was sold, I believe.'

'Did your uncle leave you any money?'

'I don't think there was any by that time.'

'What about the cousins you spoke of – do you ever see them?'

He laughed. 'Goodness no.'

They walked back along the dark quay. It was late. But there was still one light left, the bar that Colm had become particularly attached to, the one with the pin-ball machine.

'Let's have a drink,' he said. He found it difficult to go to bed while there was still anyone else left awake. It was only late at night, when they'd been drinking, that he didn't notice whether she was tired. He was so quick and thoughtful the rest of the time it was priggish to complain. There were three or four locals in the bar watching the juke-box, which was the kind that showed you a film of the person singing while their record played. He ordered two brandies and began to talk to the man next to him, a fisherman, asking about catches and so on. Beatrix noticed suddenly that he was drunk, some light in his face had gone out, he'd turned puffy, and was taking a long time over his sentences, even in English. He ordered two more brandies and she said No, not for her.

'And Colm . . . don't have another.'

He turned on her so quickly that for a second she thought he was going to hit her: his face heavy and cold. Then he turned back again to the bar and paid for his second glass.

'Let's have a game on the machine,' she said. Normally he beat her easily, but now she wasn't sure he could. The locals gathered round and she did beat him, his reflexes on the flipper buttons were so slow. They played three more times and she won them all. He stood over the machine with his head bent, astonished.

'I must be drunk!' he said, not believing it.

He looked at her and she nodded, beaming. 'Good Lord. . . . I see . . . that's what you're up to! But you're right – I'm pissed as a coot!'

'I hate that word!' She had him back now.

'Sorry, Miss. Pissed as a coot,' he muttered to himself, 'Good *Lord*!' and continued to be surprised all the way back to their hotel. She felt she'd won a victory; not over him, she'd no desire to do that, but she'd begun to help him. She was glad he needed help; not too much, but a little.

That had been last night and now their bodies were slowly changing colour on the beach while he murmured hazily about Leibnitz. Every day the sun noticeably increased in strength, but they still had the place more or less to themselves.

'I'm hungry.'

'So am I,' said Beatrix, moving the hat from her eyes, the sun hurting through her lids.

They moved to collect their picnic tucked behind a rock, Colm putting on his blue shirt and coloured trousers.

'I'm not really cut out for beach life,' he said hopefully, standing where she could see him.

'You look marvellous,' she said.

'Really?'

In fact he did look good, but not at home on a beach; she would have been disappointed if he had been.

'You know what you remind me of?' he said.

'I'm too big for a bathing-suit.'

'You'd prefer to be her?' He turned his head towards a girl at the other end of the beach where she ran a small bamboo-covered bar. In the absence of customers she spent the day horizontal on a striped mattress, slim, brown and perfect in a little white bikini.

'Yes.'

'You *fool*!' he bellowed it, sitting down at her feet in the sand as though stunned, looking up at her. She felt uncomfortable stared at from below like that, even by Colm, ever since school she'd been conscious of being larger than she wanted to be, but she made herself stand, letting him look at her. She wouldn't have minded so much if she'd been naked.

'Corny I know, but it's true. I've got to say it. I'm quite incapable of imagining a goddess who looks more like one than you do. A Northern goddess, except they're so warlike. But strong. A corny yellow goddess.'

She put a red shift over her yellow bathing-suit and tied a scarf round her head. 'My bust's too big for a bikini.'

'Aaaahh!' he made sounds of despair, shaking clenched fists in the air. 'The Health Club way you girls regard your God-given bodies! A man could be burning the topless towers of Ilium maddened by their breasts and they'd be chattering about cup-sizes.... *You're* not like that. Why pretend you are? You're *magnificent*.... Can't you get it into your head?'

'I'll try.'

They climbed the hill behind the beach to an old fort and sat under pines eating their picnic among more wild flowers than either of them had ever seen. The old moat of the fort was overgrown and at this season was like a meadow by Monet, dotted with reds and blues among the bright grape-green grasses, and a dozen shades of yellow shading from nearly white to poppy-orange, so that a shimmer of colour lay over the whole of it. After they'd eaten they lay back and listened to the insects and the birds, watching an owl flap lazily, large-winged, casting a shadow over the flowers, along the moat below them; it perched in a hole among the masonry of the fort, and then was quiet, still, almost invisible against the green and brown lichen.

'Are you getting bored?' Beatrix asked.

'You?'

'Mm? Not really.'

'I've never tried beach days before. I'm drinking too much. ... Did you say something?'

'No.'

'Ah. ... I'm not very good at holidays I think. I never feel I've done enough work to go on a holiday *from*. ... Will you live with me when we get back?'

'Yes.'

'And Sam and Cleo.'

'Colm. Is it all right?'

He raised himself on his elbow to look at her. 'All right? If I'd known when I was a boy that one day I'd meet you I wouldn't be here now. I'd have died of excitement on the way.'

'... Will you help me with Simon?'

'If you want me to,' he said 'and if you'll show me how. I'll try.' He lay back, eyes closed.

She tried not to think of Simon, tried not to think how easy it was to forget him. Yet not forget. All that had gone before was her, Simon was her; and with herself, to Colm, she brought her Simon-life. The present wouldn't prosper if it was allowed to murder the past.

She watched the owl that was now being mobbed by sparrows, blinking slowly, not moving. The sparrows kept rushing it, twittering, and then dashing out of harm's way. They reminded her of the people on the yacht, they functioned in groups, whereas the owl didn't need other owls to tell him who he was. He ignored them for a while but now he seemed to have had enough; cumbersome, indifferent, he squared his shoulders like a diver and toppled off his niche, beat his way slowly on down the moat while the sparrows shouted behind him.

'Probably couldn't see very well in the daylight,' Colm murmured. 'Out of his element. The sparrows knew that.' She hadn't realized he'd been watching. He'd known the yacht was not his element. Not that he was an owl, he was too tense and in some ways too uncertain, but he had no business among those sparrows. For all their restless darting about he had more life in him than all of them put together. She loved him for knowing where he didn't belong, for having chosen.

They gathered up the remains of their picnic and climbed

down the hill. Even the cicadas seemed to have gone to sleep. Occasionally one started off by itself but soon tailed off as though overcome by the afternoon. At the bottom of the hill the only movements in the burning three o'clock were some women doing their washing in a shaded communal wash-tub at the edge of the town. They stopped to watch them.

'What do they make of us?' said Colm. 'They're on one side and we're on the other, the same side as the yachts as far as they're concerned. Our fine shades are invisible to them.'

'If it'll make any difference I'll do your washing in our room.'

He laughed. 'I'm on the side of the washerwomen and I don't know a single one. Except you, Marie Antoinette.'

'Would you still feel the same if they had washing-machines?'

'Now *now*! Of course I would.'

'And yachts?'

'The point of yachts is there aren't enough to go round. Interesting thought though. The whole population of the Mediterranean taking to their boats, taking over each others' towns. There'd be a lot of damage.'

'To the boats?'

'To the towns. Boredom. What's the *use*, after a while, of being in somebody else's town? That's why the yacht friends have to work so hard at pleasure. As a matter of fact, if done with style, the pleasure-life could be fine; seldom is though. That's why I'm on the side of the washerwomen – I'm not making them represent anything, really I'm not – but they have a reason for being here whereas we and the yachts haven't. Not a good enough one anyway.

'To go skimming over the surface of the world ignoring the people underneath while they ignore you – it's not good for us. Don't you think? A sort of poison. Though it's not easy to see what to do about it.'

'What do you do?'

He looked quickly at her, 'I write music which the washerwomen will never hear.'

She did something she saved for the moments when she couldn't help herself: she put her arms round him and kissed him with all her heart. At these times when he followed his simplicities until he found them dangling loose in his hand he looked so vulnerable, so lost in impossibility, that to her he seemed very fine. When she kissed him he resisted slightly, suspecting patronage, but after a moment he saw there wasn't any.

Colm told her he felt as the president of the Flat Earth Society might feel if he found himself in fact at the edge of the world looking down: astonished, justified and a little appalled. So it is really true! That he couldn't remember why or when he'd first decided to hitch his wagon to that particular star – a requited human love about which he could feel no doubts. A common enough dream certainly, but he'd earned his campaign ribbons by rejecting anything less than the thing itself. And here it was. ... He didn't feel a sense of let-down as he planted his flag at the edge of the world but, also like the Flat Earth president, he could hear his voice go reedy as he returned to tell of his discovery, saw the yawns of boredom. He had no doubt that what had come, invited, into his life (whatever the practical outcome between them might be, he was careful to add that) was an intimation of something astonishing inside us; Heaven perhaps – and where else but inside us could 'heaven' ever have been?

Later that afternoon, at the beginning of twilight, he got up and half-opened the shutters, squinting up at the swifts in the now turquoise sky, wheeling and shrieking, high; it would be hot again tomorrow. Beatrix watched him from the bed, noticed how he always gravitated to windows, liked to talk back into the room while he looked out.

He was staring up at the swifts, fascinated. 'We've been squabbling about the wrong thing for five thousand years.' She said nothing, only enjoying his voice, still warm with sleep. 'You awake?'

'Sort of.'

'Mind and body – they're not separate at all. The problem isn't to bring them together – it's to stop ourselves pulling them apart.'

'Ah!' She wagged her chin up and down, her head still on the pillow. 'Ah!'.

'Madam knew that already, of course.'

'Of course. We women.'

'What blood-knowledge! The Mothers!'

'Ah!' She sat up, stretching, she was naked.

He turned and looked at her. 'And Tertullian called women "bags of excrement".'

She laughed. 'Really, the things they taught you at that boarding school! He was probably cross because he was finding it difficult to live alone.'

'With you it's as though all the bits of me are working together. Almost.'

'Almost?'

'Always "almost".' He said it gently, afraid of disappointing her.

'I think I like that best of all,' she said, 'that almost. That there's always something more, not just for you and me but for everybody if we follow the right bits of ourselves, maybe even if we don't. It's like getting warm, getting nearer something that's waiting, like a promise.'

He came over to the bed and squatted in front of her, looking up anxiously.

'It doesn't make you restless, that something more?'

'Not now. I feel I've started. Nothing bad can happen to us now.'

'Oh, it can! It can!' It came out of him like a cry, almost a sob, he tried to pull away but she held him as hard as she could and while she held him she realized what she'd been trying to say: That she was happy, perfectly happy, and if you've been like that even for a moment you believe it'll stay with you afterwards, always, like a clue.

Next morning they were woken by muffled explosions, like padded doors being slammed.

'Guns!' shouted Colm, jumping out of bed. 'I hate *guns*!' He stuck his head out of the window. 'Can't see a thing.'

Then there was a thin piping sound, a tune accompanied by a rattle of small drums. It came nearer and she joined him at the window.

Round the corner, playing a fife, came a thin fisherman in a battered three-cornered hat accompanied by two serious-faced small boys banging drums, dressed as he was in white cotton trousers, frogged military coats covered in patches and eighteenth-century hats; they all wore ordinary socks and shoes. The trousers of one boy were much too long, the other's were too short – they should have swopped. The little group called at each house, leaving out the ones that belonged to foreigners. Then they disappeared, could be heard playing and continuing their visits round the corner. From somewhere else in the town the banging continued.

They dressed and went towards the noise, seeing clouds of white smoke. The town was empty until they came under the arch into the main square. This was lined on three sides by prune-coloured fishermen of all ages, all the working men of the town, in blue military coats like the flute-player's, in white trousers, with red plumes in their tricorne hats and each armed with a villainous looking musket; the square reeked of gunpowder. On the open side on a kind of bier buried in flowers was a coloured bust of a swarthy man with a long curling moustache. He had a tin crown askew and behind the bier a priest read his breviary with cotton-wool in his ears. The only spectators were the shopkeepers, also with their ears blocked.

'It's the old boy himself. It must be. I didn't know there really was a saint of this place did you? . . . Look at this chap.'

A tall man in black and white, wearing a fore-and-aft hat with white ostrich plumes like a colonial governor's (his cotton trousers were also shrunk to six inches above his ordinary black shoes), accompanied by a tiny boy dressed the same who imitated all his movements exactly, conducted the whole proceedings with slow rhythmless motions of a cutlass. He carved the air solemnly, apparently without pattern, but there must have been one because at a certain motion the fishermen, who looked like sweating extras in a costume movie, stuffed powder down their muskets, wadded it with paper, and at certain other motions, blasted off more or less together at the now charred and jumping cobblestones. The noise was tremendous. Their hands were black with powder burns. Then at some mysterious beat in the waving of the governor's sword (mirrored by his tiny adjutant) they began to file past the statue and one by one give him a private blast at the ground in front of him until it smoked. One old man's gun failed to go off and he shook his head apologetically at the priest (or the statue) and moved on muttering, peering reproachfully down the barrel. He caught up with the man in front and they both shook the offending gun, arguing, then it went off and they disappeared in a cloud of white smoke. When it cleared they emerged none the worse and the old man, pleased, began stuffing more powder into it, and paper; the square was littered with burnt wads of it.

'I wonder how many shoot themselves?' said Colm, but he was excited. It was a beautiful sight, the colours of the plumes and the uniforms, the flashes, the smoke, the noise, the flowers (real ones, not porcelain). But what was most beautiful of all was the casual order imposed by the governor's sword – the matter-of-fact seriousness of everyone who took part. This was important to them and clearly they had done it many times before. Equally obviously they were doing it for nobody but themselves.

They watched for an hour, the same pattern over and over, Oriental in its tireless repetitiveness. Apart from anything else it was extremely hard work for the musketeers, with their ancient dangerous weapons; they were now black to the elbow, and their faces were going black, their eyes watering.

From an apologetic barber who first had to remove his plastic earplugs they learned that this was the *Bravade*, celebration of the town's final rescue from pirates in the eighteenth century which in some way the townsfolk attributed to this saint who had been a Roman centurion. The barber was contemptuous and refused to watch. 'It's the old people,' he said. 'But there are young ones there too?' Beatrix insisted. 'They follow their fathers,' he said, 'and the priest,' disposing of the matter.

It went on all day, and most of the night. The stamina was unbelievable. People love letting off bangs, but not for sixteen hard hours. There was something serious in this. Every house in the town had an image of the saint in its window, covered in the marvellous spring flowers they had seen, and old, brightly-coloured damask decorated every window-sill. The old town was ablaze with colour and flowers. Only the newer shopkeepers held aloof. Understandably; what few visitors there had been in the town had disappeared, had taken to the hills and the yachts had all gone from the harbour. It was impossible to sleep. Colm went out late to watch them again, scarcely believing they could still be at it. He came back elated.

'They had midnight mass – all in their uniforms, muskets piled at the door. And they sang wild-sounding tunes, bellowed them, conducted by that boss-man, he conducted from the altar with a *sword*! They all kept their hats on, a mass of moulting red plumes. Then when midnight came all these hoary fishermen kissed their neighbours and cried, really cried, because the mass was to commemorate all those who were with them last year and aren't there tonight. That's something like!' It seemed to make up for the porcelain wreaths; Colm was overjoyed. 'And there's a procession tomorrow up some hill. We must go.'

In the morning the stone slabs in the little fishmarket were covered in drifts of flowers, carnations, cornflowers, arranged so naturally they looked as though they grew there. This time the statue was a full-length one with a chipped toy yacht stuck under its plaster arm presumably to remind the saint of the livelihood of the people he was meant to protect. The women were exquisite in eighteenth-century country dress themselves now, faded pink and brown with yellowed lace, lovingly ironed and mended. No bangs this time, but the guns were there with sprigs of yellow and white freesia in their wide muzzles. The procession, led by the colonial governor with dark circles under his eyes by now, as well he might have, wound up a dusty road to a small chapel of St Catherine on a hill. It was hung with *ex voto* paintings of shipwrecks, thanks for rescue therefrom, chains worn by captives of the Moors and so on, the place was dusty, some of the little pictures hanging crooked, it was obviously only used on special occasions. They followed at a respectful distance, the only strangers. In the chapel it was the women's turn and they too sang, in harsh full-lunged nasal voices like Spanish women, very loud. Standing outside, Beatrix heard what Colm had meant when he had said 'barbaric tunes'; the hymns were not pleas for help but triumphant chants of shared defiance, the walls of the tiny chapel shaking. Then there was a picnic in the sun, under the shade of fruit trees, wine, children – hats, belts and muskets laid aside – little boys trying out the drums and strutting with the guns. Afterwards they all processed down the hill again, calling at more chapels briefly, only the men going in, beflowered guns on their shoulders. And then the Captain, the colonial governor in his ostrich plumes, it seemed on impulse, took the hand of a little girl who was skipping down the hill in her Boucher dress and began to skip himself, his cotton trousers flapping high above his dusty shoes. The others slowly followed suit, a ripple went down the procession, the men behind him joined hands with whoever was nearest and skipped after him, and the women and girls, all the way down the hill. When Colm and Beatrix got back to the town the flowers were gone, the fishmarket was full of fish again and the women out of their long dresses behind their stalls.

They stopped at the first bar – they hadn't had a picnic.

'Has anyone ever been so celebrated?' said Colm.

Beatrix was relieved. She'd feared he might have seen some self-consciousness in it that she hadn't noticed. She was very moved by what she had seen and for the moment wanted it left alone.

'You don't think the priests and the statues . . . ?'

'That's your Protestant upbringing.'

She was nettled. 'I don't think I *was* brought up Protestant – or any particular way come to that.'

'English then. The most materialistic race on earth froths at the sight of plaster saints.'

'Who was it told me that one of the favourites of Ireland was Saint Philomena and she never existed; the priests have had to hide her statues?'

'Can't think. Some subversive. Me? Wasn't it beautiful?'

'Marvellous. D'you think it'll last much longer?'

'It's alive now. For all we know the uniforms were left by some nineteenth-century collector who invented the whole thing. It wouldn't make any difference – we need ceremonies and they celebrated everything, their past, their dead, their being alive. I wish we could take part in something like that.'

'The barber wouldn't agree.'

'He's at the first stage of essential bloody-mindedness. That's better than trying to breathe life into dead things. Let's leave

Morris dancing alone – and let us no longer Thole the Assize.'

'Thole the *what?*'

'Really. I saw a picture of them at it. An old Anglo-Thaxon cuthtom. We need ceremonies – the one way to make sure they don't naturally get born is by hanging on to dead ones. That's why I'm pleased to have seen this. Whatever its origins, they've made it theirs.'

'What happens though when religion completely dies out? Do they all have to become like the shopkeepers, thinking it old-fashioned?'

'They have to work it out like everybody else. If keeping shop keeps them happy full stop, well and good. If not they'll find something.'

'We don't seem very good at finding things.'

'Not very.'

'Priests? What you call my "upbringing" makes me suspicious of priests.'

'As a caste perhaps. Supported by the community to turn the prayer wheel and think in peace. Not bicycling about checking that Mrs O'Grady isn't reading Plato.'

'Eh?'

'He's just been banned in Ireland.'

'What about ceremonies . . . you like those.'

'They evolve. Offerings taken to the temple. Things badly need dignifying; work, death – fear.'

'You can't take a packet of rivets to the temple.'

'Perhaps not.'

'What can you do then?'

He made a gesture of impatience, with his sandwich. 'Put a pile of them together, call it a yacht, climb inside and sail as far as possible from the people who made it I suppose. I don't know. We're working on it. Give us another thousand years.'

'Do you believe in God?'

'Oh yes. Do you?'

She nodded.

'Why?'

'I don't know. Mental laziness I expect.'

He laughed. 'You couldn't do anything else. We're given such marvellous clues sometimes.' He stood up, looking at her. 'You. For a bit anyway. We're not meant to be content. But we *are* meant to be happy.'

When they got back to the town the few visitors had returned, plus new ones, the fine spell was thought to have come to stay, and the yachts were back in the harbour. They had a swim at the small beach and on the way back stopped for a coffee at the bar on the front. Rosencrantz and Guildenstern were passing and saw them.

'Hold on to your hat,' said Colm, 'here come the Windowless Monads.'

They came in. 'What did you do yesterday and last night? We were tipped off and weighed anchor smartish.'

'It wasn't so bad,' said Colm, and Beatrix crossed her fingers.

'What was it all about?'

He explained.

'Très folk lorique.'

'It was a bit.'

'And what was that thing they carried they kept shooting at?'

'That was the great man himself.'

'General de Gaulle?'

'Madame de Gaulle, more like,' said Guildenstern.

'The local saint.'

'Trust the patron saint of this place to be a *male*!' and they both laughed.

'What do you mean?' said Beatrix, feeling it was time she intervened.

'That Tahiti beach is the centre of the trade.'

She knew what they meant but wasn't sure if Colm did.

'You see the most gorgeous sights!'

'Gorgeous whats?' said G., and they both laughed and shushed themselves.

'Why don't you come?' he said, addressing Colm, 'We'd like to see more of you ...' winking at Beatrix.

'When do you go there?' asked Colm.

'Just before lunch is the best time.'

'O.K. Hope to see you. Come on, Beatrix – we'll be late for benediction.'

Outside she said 'Late for *what?*'

'Had to say something. They're not a bad double-act those two.'

'You *are* in a good humour.'

'The thin one rather fancied me, didn't you think?' he said delighted.

'It's those trousers.'

'What's this beach they were talking about?'

'I think it's where people don't wear any clothes.'

'*Really?* . . . Girls too?'

'I think so, yes.'

'Oh, we must go!'

'Well . . .' She didn't fancy herself among the neat nymphs with taut brown skins like Latex.

'Oh come on. . . . I admit I want to stare at the girls. It's always been my ambition to be surrounded by thousands of incredibly sensual naked ladies. If it'll make you feel any better I'll confess to a sociological interest as well.'

She sighed; she would be embarrassed, but why not. 'All right.'

'Good. And let's go *after* lunch. Obviously the Monads grow Windows on that beach. We don't want them misting up.'

She was curious herself. She'd always been intrigued, even excited, by the interest men took in such things; grateful too. It was good to know that one possessed so easy a means of catching their attention. Simon at one stage had become fascinated by strip-shows and had taken her to one; she had come nearly to see the point of them (although she thought if she'd been a man she would have found them unsatisfactory), there was a mystery in impersonal nakedness and she had caught a tremor of it by proxy from the men's rapt faces. Simon had even thought of starting a club himself. 'After all – it's Instant Theatre!'

Next afternoon they took a taxi from the harbour across to the other side of the headland. They arrived at a very smart beach indeed; a palm-shaded restaurant, rows of expensive-looking mattresses with people going chocolate-colour on them, long drinks by their sides in the shade of huge blue and white umbrellas. These all wore bathing-suits.

'It's a solipsist paradise,' said Colm.

'You're always making moral judgements!' But the rows of unmoving sun-worshippers did look dispiriting.

'If one is entitled to one's enthusiasms one is also entitled to one's disgusts,' he said airily.

About a mile along the curving white beach there was another brown cluster of people. The nudists, they presumed.

'Can you make it?'

'Suppose so.' They looked a long way away and she was beginning to be irritated by this unconcealed eagerness. They took their shoes off to walk along the hard wet sand at the sea's edge.

A man and a woman were walking towards them from the far group. As they came nearer they turned into the first naked strangers either of them had ever see (outside a theatre anyway). The woman was fairly fat, middle-aged, after a second her nakedness was irrelevant but not unpleasant. It was the man who was astonishing. So much so that neither of them said anything about it till later. Beatrix was so puzzled she couldn't resist. 'D'you remember the man we first saw?' she said. 'It – seemed to come down nearly to his knees.' It had, like a length of waxy-yellow hose-pipe. 'I didn't know that was possible.' 'Neither did I,' said Colm. 'Gave me a turn. I've felt half the man since.' He considered. 'No, a quarter.' It had given Beatrix a turn too, but at the time they had walked on in silence.

Then they came upon a knot of stark-naked people gathered round a dead fish. The proud fisherman wore goggles, an aqualung and nothing else. They were all huddled together, staring down, men, women, boys, girls, distinguishable only by genitals and breasts. There was a sense of butcher's meat about so much exposed flesh rubbing together meaninglessly. One young girl at the edge of the group was jumping up and down excitedly, her breasts bouncing up to her collar-bone, which seemed to be the reason for her jumping. But one very beautiful girl stood apart, considering the sea, dark and tall. She looked Italian.

'How fantastic pubic hair is,' said Colm. He'd forgotten to breathe, he was staring so hard, as though trying to touch with his eyes. 'If you painted that girl and left it out you'd unbalance the whole design.' True.

They found a place to lie down a little way from the rest.

'It seems rather mean to keep our clothes on,' he said so they took theirs off – Beatrix was by now resigned to the idea that this was his treat. 'You look so naked compared to the others,' he said. 'I'm glad.' It wasn't too bad, Beatrix found, lying there together. So long as she didn't have to walk about. She noticed some of the girls walked about a good deal. So did Colm notice, propped on his elbow.

But for the most part the girls were wasting their time. The men who stood up oiling themselves were looking at each other. These seemed mostly to be Germans and were thorough in their inspection, had brought binoculars although nobody was more than fifty feet from his neighbour. Two diligently filmed the proceedings with ciné-cameras.

'It's clear why the Monads like this beach. It's more for them than it is for you, I'm afraid,' said Beatrix.

'Oh, I don't know. There was that girl we saw as we arrived. And that one over there. It's very odd the fascination, isn't it? Silly question I suppose.' He sighed and lay back on the sand but sat up again, in case he missed something. What *was* he looking for? she wondered.

'What on earth do I expect to see?' he said obediently.

A tall man was standing over a prone girl, talking politely. Perhaps they shared the same hotel. Absent-mindedly he tapped his bare side, obviously looking for a cigarette. He said some thing, squatting beside her, and she knelt up to rummage in her handbag, presenting her hindquarters to his social smile. Then they both stood up, shared a light, the girl sticking her handbag between her legs to have both hands free to shield the match.

'It's grotesque!' exclaimed Colm. 'Well worth coming. I've often thought "off, off you lendings!" In fact, when people are naked in public you see them less well, not better. I shouldn't be surprised if we all began to eat each other. The faces disappear.'

'Perhaps you're looking elsewhere.'

'Maybe. But to behave as though having no clothes on is natural is the most unnatural thing I've ever seen. I'd never have guessed that.' Beatrix would have. 'I think nakedness should be kept for special occasions.'

'So do I.'

'How beautiful girls are though!' he sighed. 'I'd like 'em all. ... Good Heavens!' He peered to their left. 'It can't be!' Then he stood up. He too looked naked, white, Northern, like a drawing by Blake, grains of sand on his behind, his ears pink, the sun making them semi-translucent. 'It *is*!' He sat down, stunned. 'Good Lord!'

'What are you talking about?'

'Over there. Findus! My boss. ... And a woman.'

'What do you mean – "And a woman" – maybe it's Mrs Findus?'

'She can't be – she's too. ... Hell! I think he's seen us.'

Beatrix, still lying flat, squinted sideways and saw a round middle-aged man in spectacles standing up and looking towards them. He waved.

'Well – aren't you going to wave back?'

'I suppose so.'

Beatrix enjoyed seeing him so rattled. 'He's coming over. I've told you about him,' he said quickly. 'So this is the holiday he was planning!' The man came towards them, beaming, swinging his arms carefully as though resisting, at every step, the desire to shield himself with his hands.

'I *thought* it was!' he called out. 'So, Colm, you've found our Garden of Eden.' He squatted on his haunches beaming at Colm, his spectacles glinting. Colm gruffly introduced them and Beatrix felt Mr Findus looked at her as briefly as possible. But she also felt he was having difficulty stopping his expression becoming like the ones she'd seen among the audience of the strip-show. His eyes flicked from her vaguely back to the sea. She would have preferred him to stare outright and get it over. 'How pleasant to meet in such – circumstances!' he said heartily, and Colm agreed politely. She guessed he was disconcerted, as she was, at the thought that they would soon have to walk over and meet Mrs Findus (for, it turned out, so she was), pretending, like the German they had watched, that nothing was odd. Besides, for the last quarter of an hour the sky had been thickening, greying, and there was an irritating, unpredictable wind that gusted up the dry sand, blowing it into their eyes, stinging their bodies. Most of the other people on the beach had retreated to the scrubby hollows of the dunes behind them where they lay like snipers, peering at each other through dry dirty glasses. It was time to call it a day. Nevertheless, walk across they did, Findus talking to Colm about politics as though they'd never left off, Beatrix making herself stand upright, trying not to be too self-conscious, having had more than enough of the whole experience.

They were both relieved when they met Mrs Findus. Colm because she was quiet and good-looking, Beatrix because she admired the way she greeted them, half-raising herself, a little apologetic, embarrassed, but most of all amused. Beatrix found herself hoping that one day she might be equally self-possessed.

'Margaret – this is Beatrix – ah – Pelham. Colm Treacey – whom I've told you about.' Margaret made Beatrix welcome at her side and they both lay back with relief, not talking, the situation made polite exchange absurd. They listened vaguely while the men's voices washed over them. It was the men, for whom this naked charade contained the most interest, who insisted on pretending there was nothing strange. Charles did most of the talking, his pudgy hands folded across the creases in his stomach. Both men sat facing the sea, to the side and a little in front of the women. Colm had his knees drawn up, his chin resting on them, his arms round his ankles. This was clever of him, Beatrix thought, it was both natural and protected. He looked like a boy, his hair lightened by the sun, his face reddish-brown. She noticed how narrow his hips were by the side of the older man's.

'You may ask, my dear Colm, "Why, when I have rejected my own Sacred Books, should I accept the doctrine of historical conditioning set forth by a middle-class German Jew in the nineteenth century? What about *his* conditioning? Why should I believe him, or Lenin's interpretation?"'

'Or Stalin's.'

Findus clicked his tongue reproachfully. 'Unworthy of you. I promise I shall not mention the Inquisition, Galileo, or any other historical crassness committed in the name of the Unknown to which you so valiantly cling. Let's keep the discussion on an abstract level that we can check, however, against our own experience.'

Making this little speech, wholly good natured but somewhat absently, Charles's eyes, his head turned slightly, had become fixed on Beatrix. She first realized this from a small thickening in his voice, like that of a gramophone running down. She looked in his direction out of the corner of her eye, still lying flat, and she saw his stare, became embarrassed for him because he looked at any moment likely to forget what he was talking about and fall silent with his mouth open. She glanced at Margaret, hoping she hadn't noticed, but she too was looking at her husband, a small flush on her face. He did fall silent, made a slight movement, and then, as though coming to himself, reached quickly for a towel and threw it across his lap. Unintentionally the eyes of Margaret and Beatrix met, Beatrix also blushing now, and Margaret's eyes widened; slowly, silently she began to shake with laughter; Beatrix caught it, soon they were both gasping like schoolgirls, they couldn't stop. Colm had noticed nothing, staring out to sea, he turned to them. Charles, eyebrows raised, surely (Beatrix thought) guessing, brazened it out, pretending not to understand. Their laughter increased, they were helpless, Charles muttered something mock-pompous about 'unseemly mirth' and Margaret gasped, her breasts shaking, 'No no – do go on – it's just that . . .' and they both began again.

Colm saw his chance and half stood up, his hands on the sand, still covering himself. 'It's getting a bit windy isn't it?'

'We're prepared for that, fear not,' said Charles and presumably decided it was safe to let the towel fall from his middle reached across Margaret for a green canvas contraption that unfolded into a wind-break and set it up around them. Colm sat down again sulkily. The women subsided too, exhausted, intimate as old friends.

'Well, put it this way', said Colm, impatient, he didn't enjoy this sort of argument, 'you believe in a mechanism; that man is operated on by history from outside. But I believe that something is also going on *inside* a man as well, a dynamism, not wholly explained by anything that happens outside. O.K., I'm a product of my time, my class and so on, I'm also something else. I also *have* something else, for which I am responsible to *me*. If I surrender this, I surrender my . . .'

'Soul?'

'Experience.'

'My dear boy – you believe in capital G grace ...'

'I also believe in W. G. Grace.'

'Such preoccupations are for the leisure class.' Findus was not to be teased. 'All you are afraid of, and quite rightly is being turned into a Commodity. But that is exactly the effect capitalism has now on the proletariat – I am aware these words have an old-fashioned ring. People are treated as commodities all over the world, thrown away when used.' He stared out to sea, dropping his lightly bantering tone. Now it was as if he was reciting his Credo, at tubby naked figure sitting on the sand.

'I believe that capitalism *inevitably* tends towards exploitation. I believe in social justice – which we have not got. Therefore capitalism must go. The only way to destroy so entrenched a system is to oppose it, not with goodwill but with another system stronger than itself. This is the weapon Marx laboured to forge. There may be flaws in his sword. It is the best we have. If we wish to be members of a society that does not fill us with guilt, forcing us to harden ourselves against misery, use sly little tricks to shore up our own security and protect ourselves from the apparently motiveless violence that surrounds us – motiveless forsooth! – we must work to destroy that system. And' here he spoke passionately, as though about something that worried him, 'we must be prepared for the cruelty and grotesqueness of the new. All things take time, but a new barbarism which contains hope is better than an old one from which all hope has gone.'

Colm was silent, scratching at the sand in front of him. A woman from the dunes behind walked to the sea and bent double to rinse out a coffee-pot, two red spots on her buttocks like the cheeks of a doll.

Margaret sat up slowly. 'Charles, we must go.'

'We must. Colm and Beatrix –' he glanced at her, already metaphorically back inside his clothes '– may I call you that? Forgive my lectures, *mon cœur mis à nu* – as I hope you forgive *mon corps mis* likewise. And thank you, Colm, for bringing so much beauty on to our beach.' He gave Beatrix a gracious inclination of the head. Colm was nonplussed; was he expected to say the same about Margaret? She rescued him. 'I hope you'll both come and see us in London.' She smiled at Beatrix. 'At least we can talk about clothes.' She reached for her own.

Dressed – 'That's better!' Colm muttered, pulling on his trousers – they joined up again and walked along the beach to where they could find a taxi. Margaret startled both of them by saying quietly to Colm: 'You talk like someone who believes in God.'

This irritated him. 'I believe, like the Ancient Jews, we should use that word as seldom as possible. Never perhaps.'

She was gentle but persistent: 'But why don't you say so? Are you embarrassed?'

Colm looked at her fiercely, but she wasn't trying to catch him out: she was interested.

'Not in the least. It seems to me a ridiculous and possibly dangerous formula of words – like saying "I believe in love". You know what Keats said about Wordsworth? "Every man has his own speculations, but every man does not brood and peacock over them until he makes a false coinage and deceives himself. Many a man can travel to the very bourne of Heaven, and yet want confidence to put down his half-seeing."'

'You've answered me,' she said.

'With a little help.'

The two men walked on ahead and Margaret fell behind with Beatrix. For some reason she set off the word 'Bloomsbury' in Beatrix's mind, a picture of kind intelligent ladies in shaded August orchards beating time with long fingers on the cane arms of their chairs while beautiful pre-war poets read their verses and someone came from the house calling 'strawberries?' An absurd vision, doubtless as unjust to Bloomsbury as it was to Margaret, but it contained the feel of her. The clothes she wore, old-fashioned perhaps but really dateless, unshaped silk prints of reds and blues, suited her, and she wore a large blue straw hat shading her face. They walked in silence, slowly, still companionable with their shared laughter, and every so often Charles looked back and she waved to show they were all right. Beatrix, who had never had a mother in any real sense, felt that one day she might like to talk to Margaret.

When they reached the shadowy restaurant they found the

browning bodies still turning on the spits of their mattresses in spite of the grey sky, and silent waiters still moved among them with misted drinks. Beatrix would have liked to stop there for a while, but Charles said, 'This *is* a Sunday supplement sort of place,' and she had a moment of impatience with these men who brought their preconceptions into everything and thereby spoilt a great deal. They found a taxi from the rank that waited under bamboo shade behind the restaurant and settled themselves into it, Margaret and Beatrix on the seat, Colm and Charles on tip-ups with their backs to them. Charles was now in green tweed and brown boots: Beatrix could imagine how relieved he must be to take off such clothes. Colm was laying himself out to amuse him, perhaps to avoid any further religious interrogations. He could work himself into a freewheeling Irish cycle of exaggeration that Beatrix enjoyed watching. He had taken up Charles's remarks about Sunday supplements.

'They don't only go in for holiday tips and interior decoration you know –'

'And delicious recipes.'

'They have a serious purpose as well. I have one at home I kept. It's chiefly about children growing up, informed stuff, with pictures – at the age of fifteen months some children begin to walk, Left. Picture of child with one foot in front of other. Some children cry when they think they have been deprived of their mother. Right. Half-page picture of a little girl crying. Next week. Adolescence.'

'The plot thickens.'

'After eight pages of this – five blurred blown-up photographs of the victims of the Boston Strangler.'

Charles whinnied with laughter, his spectacles flashing. 'Something for the tired parent. Masterly editing. No recipes?'

'Of course. Two pages by a lady described by Auden as "the best prose writer in America". Her subject is candlelit suppers provided by lone men for lone ladies. As their sole object must be, as she puts it, "to get a girl into the hay", she counsels the kind and amount of drink it is advisable to take beforehand in order, naturally, to circumvent this. She was very cheery though. She reckoned to be able to put away a bottle of champagne "from one of the really great years" (I quote) and still go burping home in a taxi while her host gnashed his teeth over the washing-up.'

Beatrix had never heard anyone chortle, but that is what Charles seemed to do, stamping his boots on the floor of the taxi. 'One begins to understand the Boston Strangler.'

The taxi stopped in the town square, the cobbles still charred by the muskets, the men had an amiable tussle over who should pay for the taxi, Charles yielding, and they stood awkwardly saying good-bye.

'You must come and see us,' said Margaret again. Then to Beatrix, 'See me at any rate.' She took her hand as though to shake it. 'You are very beautiful.' She said it simply, a statement of fact.

'So are you,' Beatrix blurted out foolishly, because it was true and because she was put off balance by the poise of the older woman. Margaret heard but gave no sign that she had. 'Do come and see me,' she said and let go her hand. Beatrix knew that she would.

'We must rejoin our friend up the hill – he's rather a recluse I'm afraid,' said Charles.

'We're leaving ourselves tomorrow,' said Colm. Findus had become shifty, none of them wanted to spend the rest of the day together.

'Ah. Until the prison-house then?'

They watched the older couple walk away across the square, Margaret taking Charles's arm; Beatrix realized she had half expected it to be the other way about.

'What an extraordinary woman!' said Colm.

'Did you like her?'

'Yes. But I'll have to re-think my Findus.'

'I don't think I really like the nudist beach. Sand blowing up my nose. Up my everything.'

'Why on earth do I want to look at naked girls when I have you? It's like a disease men have – a part of us is undifferentiated lust. Do girls feel that?'

'I expect so. Not quite in the same way, maybe.'

'Do you?'

'Not at the moment.'

It was nearly dusk; the sun went very quickly. The sky had

cleared again and bats were making an air-canal of the narrow street they were walking down.

'I'd have liked to stop a bit at that smart restaurant. It looked so pretty.'

'Findus was so scathing I guessed he couldn't afford it.' He paused. 'I've never done that before: not stopped somewhere because another person couldn't afford it. Either we all couldn't or the one who could paid. It's the Beatrix millions. They're confusing me.'

She said nothing. She wasn't going to play mother – not to him – not, anyway, past the point of motherliness and fatherliness that we all owe sometimes to people we love.

Much later, the town asleep, because it was their last night they walked along the narrow path, past the cemetery, some of the wreaths glinting in the moonlight, the moon itself hidden behind the black outline of the old fort above them. They stood on the beach and small waves slapped the sand, still disturbed by the memory of the morning wind, showing little white combs of foam. Apart from these everything was still. She asked him about Findus.

'Most men of his age are looking back at an idealized past. He idealizes the future. I like that.'

'But doesn't it all seem a bit – simple?'

'He's on a quest. Most quests look simple from outside. I know mine does.'

'But what about the awful things?' This had been worrying Beatrix since the morning; too much had been left unsaid. 'What about writers and people being arrested? And that awful wall in Berlin, people being shot when they're stuck in the barbed wire?'

'A Slav interpretation has Slav history behind it. Writers were arrested under the Czars, people were shot down outside the gates of the palace when they'd come unarmed to ask for bread. History moves in circles. But there's no need to suppose that Communism in Britain would revert to the days of King John.'

'But surely it's wrong to put up with wicked things now for the sake of good things in the future?'

'There are wicked things in our way too – only we're used to them.... You're right though.'

'But you gave the impression you thought he was.'

Colm had picked up some stones and was trying to bounce them on the sea. Each time they hit the water they threw up a small splash of white, almost phosphorescent, but it was the light of the moon behind them.

He threw another. It bounced three times. 'I do think he's right,' he said. 'And so am I. And I think my way –' he threw again and this one bounced five times before it sank; he made sure it wasn't going to reappear before he went on, 'has more future to it. But that's up to me to prove.... No it isn't.'

He turned to her, one hand cupped full of stones against his chest. She thought afterwards how like him it was to say what he did when he couldn't touch her.

'Beatrix, as you know, all my life I've believed in something not very original. Very simple certainty. The possibility of loving another person, because I thought it might throw a light on life, more than a personal light. It was a desire – a memory – of a vast and simple happiness. I believed this was possible although I had no experience of it and saw no convincing evidence of it in other people. So I believed in something I could not see. I felt the strength of my belief was a guarantee that it did exist. People have argued for the existence of God like that, and other people have laughed. Quite rightly. I also knew there was little I could do to help me find what I was looking for except to say No to all that was less. This I did. Well – I was right. It does exist. It has happened. Nothing remains to be proved. I love you. Anything that might go wrong between us through my stupidity or bad luck or time or all three can't prove that what I felt to be in the world is not there. This changes everything. Nothing is solved but now there is a reason. Everything remains to be done in the light of it.'

He made this speech standing on the stones of the beach with the ones he had picked up still in his hand. Beatrix listened to him and the small splash of the waves behind.

He let the stones fall as though he'd forgotten them and either because of the stillness of the night or because of what he had said Beatrix heard them drop individually, with no clatter, as though they fell one by one like stone feathers.

He came and stood in front of her and she smelt the sun on his skin as they stood in the dark. He leaned his forehead on hers, only the bones keeping each other out, and through his hair she saw Orion's belt, faint in the moonlit sky, infinitely far, an infinite time, away.

Walking back, again past the glinting cemetery, he was gayer than she had ever seen him.

'I feel like Chinese boxes,' she said. 'We're the smallest one in the middle and we'll try to grow to meet the size of the other boxes one by one.'

He laughed. 'Now do you see why I believe in God? Because of you.'

'But I'm not God!'

'Thank God!'

Next day they went back to London.

9

When they arrived they went, without discussion, to Colm's flat, which Beatrix had never seen.

She was surprised: books, records, a comfortable chair or two, even some pictures. He carried their suitcases into the bedroom and she prepared herself for a pang at the sight of his sad single bed. She experienced another sort of pang, equally foolish, when she saw that his bed was more than large enough for two, with a rust-red South American poncho thrown over it. The room was pretty; before they had met he had led his life, just as she had.

She telephoned Simon, Colm disappearing, going to buy some food and drink.

Ita answered. Simon was in Manchester, had been for a week and had left a number. Yes, Sam and Cleo were fine.

Hardly knowing what she was doing, the situation, simple as it was, having passed the point of thought, but preparing herself against Simon's known capacity for turning everything into farce, she rang Manchester. It was an hotel. Eventually Simon was found.

'Bea! Darling! You're back. How was it?'

'You shouldn't have left Sam and Cleo.' *He* shouldn't . . . she wasn't making much sense.

'Well, you see it's all been rather awkward. Quite a lot has happened while you've been away. I've become a sort of telly star. They offered me this series – "Our Hideous Heritage?" – there's a question mark after that by the way – me looking at buildings regarded as NBG and saying how super they are. I've just done one actually while they were demolishing the heritage. I moved on to the next bit as the one I was talking about collapsed – "We'll have to look at this example of industrial Gothic rather quickly, I see the bulldozer coming". Crash! "Oh well.

Never mind. I expect the dust will clear in a minute and you'll be able to see me again. Please do not adjust your sets before leaving" – That sort of thing – I wear one of those yellow tin hats –'

'Simon.'

'Yes?'

'I'm at Colm's flat.'

'Oh. . . Are you going to stay there?'

As slowly as she'd heard the stones roll out of Colm's hands she heard her voice cutting the throat of her girlhood, her young womanhood. There was a pause. 'Yes, Simon.'

'I mean – for good?'

'Oh, Simon!' She was almost pleading with him now. 'How can I say I'll just live with him for a bit – see how it works out!'

He said slowly, considering this, 'No – you couldn't say that. But I mean – I'll see you again, won't I?'

'Of course! Oh – Simon I am sorry. . .' It was so foolish, like Colm when he had disappointed her, trying to shift the burden, asking for everything to be made all right. But she felt sorry. 'I had to tell you.'

'Oh yes, indeed. Well –'

'When are you coming back?'

'That's the awful thing. Not for a week or two. I'll write. And then we'll meet?'

'Of *course*!'

'Bea. . . . I'm sorry too.'

And what she dreaded would happen did, she began to cry. Unfair, unforgivable female thing to do. Her sobs increased, the call ended in confusion. Simon, appalled, trying to reassure her, Beatrix unable to get whole words out; in the end it was she who put down the receiver.

She went to Colm's mirror to do something about her face. There was no chair by the mirror; of course no dressing-table. She sat on the bed looking at their two suitcases, frightened. Was it as easy as that?

Colm came back, looked at her, and sat on the bed beside her. Then he took a bottle from a carrier-bag and gave her a drink of brandy. He went into the sitting-room and switched on the electric fire and the lamps, took her in there. Then he cooked some supper and produced a bottle of wine. They didn't talk much; not at all about Simon. Her body ached as though she had walked too far and too long. Colm was edgy, restless, trying not to be.

About eight o'clock she went to the house to see Sam and Cleo. She'd put on some armour now, which was something she should have done before. She found a note left by Simon: 'Hope you had a good time': and then at the bottom, scrawled later: 'No I don't. Love and OXO. S.' She put the note in her handbag. Sam and Cleo were not yet asleep and were, as Ita had said, fine. Sam asked her politely where she'd been, but was really waiting to tell her about his visit to the Zoo. Cleo was quiet and preoccupied as she always was. Beatrix explained to them both, she felt able to cope now, that she wouldn't be sleeping with them for a few days but that she was very near and would be with them every day as much as always. After a question or two they seemed satisfied by this. Then she explained to Ita. She felt as generals must do when ordering their men into battle; she couldn't be too concerned with the implications of what she was doing, but she was clear it had to be done.

This was the pattern of their lives for the first few weeks. A letter arrived from Simon.

'It's hard to get used to the idea, but I suppose we must, eh? I'd seen us soldiering together into the autumn of our days but now I also see that I rather took that for granted. My life gets so *absurd* ... not that it's an existential comment or anything like that. I can't blame it on the Bomb or Contemporary Whatevers. I think I've got a grasshopper mind like that poor bloke who used to feature on the back of *Reader's Digest*. (Perhaps he still does? It's a rather crafty place to advertise for the g-h-minded, come to think of it.) The fact is I haven't quite taken this in yet. I suspect it'll hit me in years and years and then you'll have a haggard Simon on your hands counselling repentance and cadging a kip in the back room.

'Talking of that – I'm going to Aussie-land for a bit – apparently they have no end of a Hideous Heritage there, poor dears. So why don't you and Colm move into the old homestead? After all, it's yours. I'd quite like to rescue some of the furniture one day, but there won't be ugly scenes about that. Look after it for me. Don't let your house-guest be sick over it. I don't think I'm cut out for marriage. Bea – you were the wrong girl to find that out on.

'God! reading this dreadful letter over I sound *relieved*. Well, I'm not. Sometimes when I think we'll never have our chats again I could weep buckets (you'd never believe how *funny* you could be when you did your clowning thing). But I mustn't go on or this'll sound like a letter read out by remorseful widow in Noel Coward play after hubby has crashed in flames. Oh, darling Bea.

'*Obscene relief note*: I've been seeing a certain amount of a certain Thin – you can only see a certain amount of her; when she turns sideways she disappears. Haw! Haw! I try, ladies, I try. *Well* – it appears or rather appeared that Thin had a Thing about your Simon. So I said to myself why not? Wife a-whoring on the continong (don't mean that) what about a bit of a cuddle for poor old Simon? In fact I couldn't resist, she's the nearest thing to nonexistence walking – what *could* it be like? Well – (again) – it was like going to bed with a boy in a trance. She's as dopey then as she is at all other times. It's a permanent state! Riveting! She's very relaxing. The evening's a howling success if she manages not to drop off. To cut the tale short, she's rather soupy about the dashing Simon. That is to say she sags about wherever I happen to be, which is spooky but good for the image. Last night I dreamed I took her to be lobotomized. The chap tapped open her head with an egg-spoon (she didn't feel a thing of course), peered inside and when he said Good Lord! his voice echoed so hollow that I woke myself up laughing. I love you, Simon.

'PS. When I think what's inside your head I see bowls of fruit and cool wine in pottery jugs, and tile-floored Greek cottages, terracotta and white, wooden furniture scrubbed yellow, coloured cloths over the cushions and tables. There! A yellow Mediterranean hausfrau. Did I ever tell you I saw you like that? I'm sure not. It sounds ghastly but isn't. X. S.'

What could she do with such a letter? It seemed false to hide it and wrong to show it to Colm and yet she had no corner of the flat which was specially hers. She left it where she originally put it down, in the corner of the bedroom where her make-up was. Colm picked it up, not thinking. 'What's this?'

'From Simon.'

He put it back so quickly she found herself saying: 'Read it if you like,' not knowing whether she wanted him to see how she was valued and how nice Simon was or whether, more innocently, she refused to keep anything from him.

He read it and carefully put it back in its envelope. He was silent and then said: 'I don't care. I want you. Wanting doesn't give us rights, but I've got you and I'm going to keep you.'

It had been wrong to show it to him; it had been a trap to make him say that.

Simon came back from Manchester and she went to see him, but he was so obviously enjoying being a celebrity that there was no time to talk. When she saw him prancing round the room in a bush-hat, the kind Australian soldiers wear, she found herself protesting as she would have done in the old days.

'Simon darling, you don't have to go as far as all that. Anyway, they'll probably want to see you in a bowler.'

'Oh, I've got one of those too.' And he took a new one from a box, curly-brimmed, clapped it on his head so that his long hair stuck out all round. He looked like something out of Ouida.

Was it sad to see the Simon she had known turning from a comedian to a clown, exploited, exploiting himself? Not really. He had complete faith in his own ability to emerge from anything, and would make sure he enjoyed himself on the way. She was saddened to find herself thinking: 'Really I left him a long time ago – only I was lazy.'

He was called for by the Canadian producer of his television show, a small man with a beard and watering eyes whom Simon introduced simply as 'The Greatest'. This was his name for him, sometimes abbreviated to 'Great' – 'Hey Great – have you got the fags?' sometimes just to 'The'. A chauffeur-driven car arrived to take them to the airport and Simon considered long and loquaciously which of his hats he ought to put on in order to take it off to kiss her good-bye while The Greatest laughed soundlessly, wiping his eyes as though sure Simon would be the death of him. Eventually he decided on the bush-hat and then he made Beatrix genuinely laugh by doing an imitation of Jacques Tati, hands behind his back, his long body bent almost in half, peering from under his bush-hat until he walked spring-heeled through the enormous car and out the other side as though he hadn't seen it. The Greatest turned to her and shrugged, his mouth turned down at the corners, as if to say 'Isn't he the greatest?' and at last they both drove off. It was a strange end.

So they left Colm's flat and went to live temporarily in the house. Colm did his best not to look like a guest among all the Simonries, which he detested. He brought his piano and installed it upstairs. He spent much of the day up there. When he came down he never talked about what he was doing and she learned not to ask him. She could tell it was going badly if his face had a look of dustiness that she wanted to wipe away. He became fascinated by the children, especially Cleo. He could sit and play with her for an hour, both of them silent. He could also make her laugh which no one had been able to do with any certainty before.

When Colm's friends came they tended to sit about awkwardly and she found herself trying too hard. It began to affect them slightly. One evening Colm, pushing himself back from the table, broke his chair; he was upset, absurdly tried to stick it together with Uhu. He wouldn't have cared if it had been his own chair. The fuss he made frightened Beatrix and she intensified her visits to estate agents, but Colm always became evasive when they went through details of houses, she couldn't be sure why.

Derek and Colm went out drinking one night. When they came back she heard them talking in the hall, laughing, but when they came into the room Derek fell silent, just smiling, until Colm lapsed into silence himself. Beatrix was furious with Derek, he even chose to sit with his overcoat on. Eventually he went and Colm came back from seeing him out:

'Good *Lord*! That was rather horrible.'

'Wasn't it.'

'Did you hear, then?'

'What?'

'Derek. In the hall. When he said good night he – well he just about congratulated me on this house: "You've done pretty well for yourself – good on you, sport".'

'Oh ...' Beatrix could have stamped with anger at the malice of it. Derek knew very well what he was doing. But she would never convince Colm of that.

'It's true, though. We've got to find a place.'

'But we're looking. I want to get out of here as much as you do. Anyway, what's true? That this house is a desirable property in Derek's eyes? So what? Your flat was nice. You didn't live in bachelor squalor before.'

'No. I don't like disorder. Stops me working.'

'Well then – what? These things we get from agents – you won't help me.'

'Partly because I'm scared. You know how clothes affect the ways you feel. Some houses can come down over your eyes like a hat. After a while you just keep on reading the hat-band. Good title for a play that – "It's a seven and one-eighth world".'

'Colm – I'd live in a hole in the ground if that's what you wanted.'

'I know.'

'What shall we do then?'

'Just – be careful.' He went to the window. 'Simon's been good – no trouble. This house – the transition with the kids apparently painless – bye bye misery! hello happiness! It's all very *bland*!'

'Would you prefer fights?'

He'd been staring out of the window at the trees in the street-lights, now he turned. 'What we'd prefer has nothing to do with it. You remember what we said about Chinese boxes? It's easy to line the first, the one we're meant to climb out of, so snugly and tightly that we can't.

'Must we go looking for difficulties then?'

'No. But there is something we have to go looking for. Have you noticed how the people round here only seem to know each other?'

She had. Simon often talked about them, laughing, but regarding it as inevitable. There was something over-snug, however – not in Simon but in the way comfort was allowed to shape their lives, instead of good fortune setting them free, allowing them to shape their own.

'What do we do then?' she said. 'Pretend I'm poor? Give it away? Or just feel guilty?'

'We could always take drugs.'

He was staring abstractedly at Simon's sofa with the men at each end. His eyes, moving away, caught hers and they both laughed.

'D'you find these questions glum?'

'No.'

'As soon as you have enough to eat they come. Nobody knows the answers. We could stay here,' he said doubtfully. 'I don't want to make you uncomfortable.'

'Ta.'

'Let's be floaters, you and me. It's a ship we're on, the whole set-up I mean. It's got a bit old and smelly but we're lucky, we can choose, so let's be deck-passengers, on the boat but outside it, then we might be able to see where we're going.'

'Is it going anywhere?'

'Er – no. It's sinking, actually.'

'And we've got to sink with it.'

'No choice. It's *us*. With any luck we might have learned to swim for ourselves by that time.'

'That sounds a bit mean.'

'On the contrary. The more of us who learn to swim for ourselves the better. It might catch on. All those passengers jumping off and happily splashing privately away might make the crew smarten up its ideas.'

'All right then.... When do we start?'

'No use waiting for the Second Coming. Now. There's nothing wrong with the houses we've been looking at except that there's nothing wrong with them. What we need is a rotten house.'

'Ah.' She let her mouth sag open and Colm raised his eyebrows like a supercilious auctioneer.

'Of course. To be reminded that we're living in a house at all. Why d'you think people go camping? Shock tactics. A week of that and they're reconciled to the mortgage.'

'Colm, you're daft.'

'Only consider, dear lady. We must set our lives with reminders, like traps against traps. Our device shall be "Remember to Remember". You wait till you see me wading in the septic tank.'

'What'll that remind you of?'

'Mortality. You know what's wrong with these architectural gems we live among? Money has been used to insulate them against the sound of snapping window-sashes.'

She'd heard that soundlessness like a ringing in her ears.

'But you won't spend too long in the septic tank, will you? What about me and –'

'I promise to change.'

'– what about your work?'

'No special insulation for people who musicalize, pictorialize or write lies, even white lies. Any more questions? . . . Because you do none of those things do you regard yourself as ungifted?'

'Yes.'

'The lady in the white cashmere shift (what is it? you look marvellous) is quite wrong. She's the most gifted human being I've ever met.'

'What with?'

'With being a human being.'

'Thank you, sir.'

'And if we find this house you'll have every chance to prove it.'

'So long as it isn't *just* me.'

'Well, of course, I shall be rather busy most of the time.'

She flicked the remains of her drink at him. He explored his chin with his tongue, looking upwards: 'Extraordinary. Even when the roof leaks in these parts it tastes of gin.' Grabbing her he whirled her through the room, dancing, pushing her, giggling, in between Simon's furniture, sliding it away with his side as they passed. 'God I love you!' he said. 'It's fantastic to have what one wants. Just you. Nothing else. That's all I want. And I've got it!'

'Not too private and cosy?' she asked, raising her eyebrows now.

'You're asking *my* questions! No. Not too private as a matter of fact. A multiplication.'

'Sure?' She leaned back to look at him, as he held her by the waist, widening her eyes still further, coyly.

'Sure I'm sure and only *I'm* allowed to laugh at me.'

Colm's indecisions could be protracted, but he moved fast once he'd discovered a formula he could, anyway for the moment, accept. He found them a house in Shepherd's Bush, on the main road ('traffic *is* this town!') but with a small garden at the back for the children. Some things needed doing to it, a new window on the dark ground-floor ('see what money can do? Buy light!') but he cut out everything she intended for him. He hated owning anything, resented anyone's need for money and possessions. When she teased him about this, because it seemed to her a form of male arrogance and made her laugh, he waved his hands and said that although there might be people who had evolved a balanced attitude to such matters he had yet to meet one. Perhaps there were some things we weren't *meant* to come to terms with. ... This wasn't a pose of his, or an illusion, he genuinely cared very little for such matters. But he tried. There was no problem of the house he was unwilling to share with her. So much so that sometimes she had to order him to leave the whole business, to go and do some work, catching the expression of relief on his face before he had time to hide it.

When he got back from his holiday Colm was given a larger office – or rather, a smaller one but with two outer offices. In the second one, next to Miss Florentine, Findus had installed his most brilliant stroke; a young man who flooded the building with memoranda. These were returned to the young man marked *Action* with a congratulatory tick from Above (Colm could imagine the dismay they must have caused, and Findus's delight) and the action he took bred, in turn, more memoranda. Colm was now required to attend the office on only two days, at the same pay, so that he could do more 'on the creative side': how Charles had managed to swing that one, how he'd even managed to phrase it to those dedicated short-hairs at the Top, remained a mystery. However – he would have to leave. No longer having to do it, financially, made this more difficult, but he decided to have the courage of his own guilt. There was a pretence about his weekly stint behind his desk that weighed him down, was in fact even more sappingly dishonest than he could define. He told Findus, who was not surprised.

Being with Beatrix was as simple as before it had seemed strange and probably impossible. He saw himself and the world in a relation more immediate than before; she helped him, just by being, to an extent which, he was certain, she had no idea, although he told her.

After they'd been together about five months, each day if anything more surprising to him than the one before, he decided to go gliding again. He rang the airfield and they told him the weather looked right.

He'd first tried gliding years before with a friend. The sensation was so private that he'd wanted to experience it on his own and so he had learnt. But he was not a good pilot and never took up a passenger, largely because the point was to be alone in mid-air but also because it didn't seem fair to risk somebody else's neck as well. He had a reputation at the Club as a daredevil because of a particularly long trip he'd made after being caught up in a thunder-cloud he hadn't noticed. He'd gone on because he hadn't known what else to do; also, in those days, he'd believed he was immortal, which was no longer the case. He enjoyed his gliding friends, their talk of 'cirrocum' and dated 'prang' parlance, the sheer joy of waving to each other from the open cockpit, all up together on a fine day, like 'Dawn Patrol'. It was an expensive business. He had no car so it meant a train to the West Country, a taxi at the other end. He did it perhaps once a year.

His club was called a bunjy club because of the way the gliders were launched there. The field was at the edge of a plateau, you were pulled on a spring to the edge and if there was a wind it hit the hill, pushed upwards, you caught it and were pushed up also. That was the idea, anyway. A primitive form of take-off but cheaper; this was not a club for cracks, which was why he liked it.

They were all there, or nearly all – 'the boys'. It was mid-week, but a surprising number could manage a day off when the weather was right; his own racket did not seem unique. It was good to see them. Nothing like ritual and a minor danger shared minus sexual competition for making a group of men feel at ease with each other. Nevertheless, Colm had usually run out of things to say by evening. He was delighted to see Toby, his great stand-by, a writer he admired who did hack-work for TV: occasionally a play of his own was put on at a non-commercial theatre; mysterious, not quite coming off, but with an unforced threatening quality, powerful devils under the suburban lawn. He and Toby drank pink gins in the old Battle of Britain mess, enjoying the travesty element but never mentioning this to each other, they were not conspirators, but they sought each other out.

Colm's turn came, Toby helping on the bunjy. There were a few clouds building up now, clean, white ones, it should be a good day. The wind caught him as he reached the edge, he released the cable, waving down to them, and he was afloat. There was indeed plenty of lift, the green pellet in the climb indicator registered a rise of about ten feet a second. He settled himself in his seat to enjoy this. One of the few similes he allowed himself from gliding was that (like life) if you weren't going up you were going down. Also he had to admit that, as in his own life, you depended on invisible pockets for support; here you kept your eyes open for a certain look of cloud, a kind of landscape, a buzzard navigating an air-stream, but really you were guessing; there was no mistaking, though, when you were sustained, or when you were let down with a bump; on ground level also there were pockets of energy waiting to be tapped, he tried to slip from one to the other, and couldn't (and didn't) complain when he fell.

The green pellet still went up, more slowly now – perfect. Below him the fields shrank into prettiness and the small clusters of Cotswold houses looked as if they were huddled together for reassurance, which they were.

Wasn't he making rather heavy weather over this house business, this box to shelter them? What more basic and natural preoccupation? Men spent their lives defining family areas with spear or cheque-book; smiling at Sir for promotion, baking dung bricks in the sun. A man he knew had written a marvellous book about a Mr Biswas – all he wanted all his life was a house. What happened in the end? ... It had been ruined anyway, swept off in a monsoon. Of course. That didn't make his ambition foolish. Why was he, Colm, so uneasy? Because he had no tribe – a meum-tuum situation outside the tribe had a tinge of meanness; a solitary scrabble with pieces of coloured paper for possession of an unconnected cave....

The aircraft leapt and slipped down, as if the rising pillar it rested on had suddenly collapsed, pulled from under him by Samson. (His friends on the ground always talked of 'us' – 'we hit a marvellous blue thermal over Daglingworth' – 'we' being self and ship. Colm could never feel that close towards the frail arrangement of wood and canvas in which he sat; at best it was indifferent, often hostile. This was probably why he would never be a good pilot.) He peered over the edge of the cockpit (the red pellet was rising now, fast, he was falling) and saw two gulls planing on the air. They ought to know what they were doing. Sure enough he found lift near them, they were in the centre of it, and he felt the power of it, like a strong hand under his behind. He'd better turn the nose. Didn't want to get too far from the field. As he banked the lift continued, this was going to be a good one.

New clouds were forming now, condensation on the tips of rapidly rising shafts of air. He turned about again to find one of these, deciding to go really high, he was enjoying himself.

The point was – life was absurd with suffering and death. Wasn't worth living if death was at the end of it. Absurd and true. Death was an outrage, horrible, always. After such movement, such stillness. Even as a boy in Ireland he'd been amazed at his cousins. Bang – and what before was a bird was now a bundle of feathers. Why didn't it freeze their blood? If not pity for the bird, then terror for themselves? But he saw nothing of the sort in their eyes. How did they manage it, ignorant as cattle?

Beatrix.

To be presented with an awareness of another life so intense seemed to say something about life itself. What? He'd been given this bonus and it was his duty to work it out. But when he tried to reach for it, stretching, he snapped back painfully inside his own skin. Each time this happened, though, he felt himself fitting inside his skin a degree more comfortably, as if he had in fact been stretched, fewer bits of him rattled about loose. To him this meant that although we must go on asking impossible questions it is unwise to go hunting too many heavenly Snarks; it was time he got full value from this world – he hadn't realized there was so much of it there. It suggested that the physical world was itself a form of allegory the full meaning of which we missed if we didn't concentrate on the literal one. It was time he took on Beatrix, with all that implied. Such an elementary and 'grown up' resolve might have come to him earlier but he had to approach such matters warily, he wanted to know at all times where he was, wherein he was being conned, conning himself.

The world said: 'Give up your foolish dreams of Elsewhere: Look at *Me*!' All right. But when you did look it was impossible not to feel it was trying to say something else, equally simple, *as well*. Because we can't quite hear does that mean nothing spoke?

However, it was the prosaic quality now that appealed to him most. He didn't feel like a Tiepolo saint, corkscrewing up to heaven. More as if he'd climbed a small rise in a flat plain, gasping rather, but excited, and for the first time was able to look round and make partial sense of what he saw. Which reminded him, he couldn't see a thing now from the glider. He'd become involved in a large cloud; easy to do, the wispy margins of some clouds are difficult to define, and now he seemed heading for the centre of it, the green pellet whizzing up alarmingly and it was growing darker. Not again! There was a yellow tinge in the centre of the cloud – don't say he'd blundered into a storm again! Then it began to hail, painfully, and he applied his airbrakes but they wouldn't budge. He tried them every few moments and they began to give slightly but not completely unstick. The indicator showed a rise of about 50 feet a second, an airspeed of 60 knots, both of which were much too fast. He tried to get the nose down and couldn't. It began unpleasantly to lighten, a sulphurous, thundery light, but as yet thank goodness there was no thunder. He tried to remember the shape of the cloud, but hadn't noticed it so couldn't guess which side of it to aim to come out of. He kept turning, trying to lose height. Meanwhile he was being shaken about badly, would suddenly go up – he shouldn't have been rude about Tiepolo's saints, you *could* be moved up very fast – and then fell with a bump that made him fear for the slender wings. He set course for the airfield, he wanted to get home tonight and he was tired of being Jove's yo-yo. It was extremely cold, but by shoving at the air-brakes he managed to dislodge some lumps of hail and get them free. Better. Now they were going down quickly. It became darker, to his comparative relief. Then he remembered there was indeed a slight rise on the plain below, a kind of tor. He'd better not go down too fast or he might hit it; but he had no choice, he was caught in a down-draught now.

He came out of the cloud; but too low. He looked back at his adversary; it was beautiful, crimson and yellow and warm smoky blue, a beautiful monster with entrails of brass. He wasn't anywhere near the small hill, but he was below the escarpment he had to reach. He looked around for some lift and found a little over a bonfire. Then he saw the glint of the reservoir and found some more over that. He was now just over the level of the field but to the east, with some trees in his approach. Should he settle for a field in the plain below? That would mean getting back very late tonight after finding a telephone, waiting for a tow. He loved his box with Beatrix in it. Although it wasn't his. Beatrix was his although she wasn't. They were each other's. Were they that? He decided to risk the airfield. He had enough height unless he hit an unlucky hole which he did. The aircraft fell vertically an essential hundred feet, but at last shuddered at the bottom and held steady, Colm gritted his teeth in sympathy with the wings. How did they take such strains? A miracle of mathematics. The kingdom of numbers. What pleasure to inhabit that certainty; he would like his music to have it, mathematical progression, ascension block by block, integer by integer until it formed a house he had made himself, one he could understand and both of them could climb inside and signal from.

The tops of the trees were now unpleasantly close to the little canvas bucket he sat in. He saw the white blobs of faces on the airfield running towards him – he wished they wouldn't do that, it made him nervous. Then he felt the first gentle touch. Damn, the fabric might be torn, the club couldn't afford a damaged glider, they'd curse him. Then he really hit and was furious because now the glider might be a total write-off and the fault was his, he should have settled for the valley. There was no danger to him, he wasn't high, or going fast enough, but gliders were more delicate, more awkwardly shaped than he was. There was the sound of a wing cracking. The cockpit seemed to turn on its side violently and he began to laugh because they'd find him dangling upside down in his harness like Toby the time he got caught in the telephone wires; then there was a bigger bump and he felt the brush of the fir trees on his face.

Toby was the first to reach him. The glider was destroyed, a wing had become wedged under the angle of a branch and the whole thing had veered round, splitting; it was one of the last trees in the wood; if he'd hit earlier, the other trees would have stopped the glider twisting like that. Colm was thrown clear, his harness had snapped, and he lay in the open field. Toby shouted 'Colm?' He was smiling, with his eyes closed. Then he stood by him while the others arrived, gathering round, falling silent. After a few moments they turned and walked back to telephone. There was no need to hurry.

Toby was given the job of going through Colm's things. A photograph of Beatrix, added to some gossip he remembered hearing, told him the person he had to see. He decided to tell her himself, wishing it didn't have to be him. He caught the train to London, the one Colm and he had planned to travel back on. When he rang the bell she would think it was Colm. But the telephone seemed impossible.

When Beatrix opened the door she thought it must be the man from the estate agents about the Shepherd's Bush house. It was an odd time in the evening, but she'd implored them to hurry; largely because she'd seen Colm looking at one of Simon's naked putti in an angle of the stairs. She had felt for him. Simon had slightly changed the painting of the face so that it had a fixed lecherous simper that might have been funny once but not a dozen times a day.

The man on the steps grinned at her uncertainly. He seemed to have a permanent wide smile that kept vanishing altogether as though he was having trouble with it. She suddenly saw that he looked like the bearer of bad news.

'Mrs Pelham?'

'Yes.'

'I'm Toby Went.'

A gliding friend of Colm's.

'Where's Colm?'

'May I come in?'

'I'm sorry. Yes, do please.'

They went into the hall, she opened the door into the sitting-room and he crossed it to the far side, moving away from her, turning by the fireplace. The gentle lines of his face seemed blurred. It was a gentle face. She heard his breathing.

'It's about Colm I came.'

'There's been an accident. Where is he?'

'It's – bad.'

She stared at him waiting for him to say more. Then she said: 'Colm is dead,' not believing it, phrasing the worst to see him shake his head. But he didn't shake it.

'Yes, my dear. He is.'

There was a small gap and then the part below her head fell away like a cliff collapsing, there was just her head left on top of an empty space, she heard the roar of the cliff falling away and the silence that followed.

'Would you like some tea?'

What time was it? Night? Why had she said that? On the kitchen table were some chops for their supper. A dishcloth was lying crumpled on a chair. Colm had helped her last night and she could never get him to hang up the cloth to dry, he was always in too much of a hurry to get them both out of the kitchen. It was still damp. She clutched the edge of the sink and the words fell separately, like stones, into the empty space under her head. No – more – Colm-ever.

Then the cliff came back with a roar, clamped itself hard into position again like a huge steel sheet with spikes that went through her and stayed, from the front to the back. Her hair felt heavy. The front of her head burning, a cold heat.

'Are you all right?'

A voice from the door. She was bent over the sink, supporting the iron spikes, so that her forehead touched the wet bottom of it. She straightened, the face at the door made way for her. They were back in the sitting-room.

'Tell me about it,' she said, taking one of Colm's cigarettes from his box. It was his, they were smoking it together, he would help her with this stranger who was talking.

She heard very little; he was describing what happened. She smoked and listened to a strange sound in her ears as though the whole house had become a shell that contained a whining, distant, rushing sound. She tried not to bend, to curl round the iron spikes – tried not to move at all in case they tore her. The man stood up.

'Is there anyone I can telephone to be with you?'

'No, thank you. I'll be all right.'

'Would you like me to stay?'

'No. Please go. Thank you.'

'I shall ring again tonight to see if you want anything. Please answer.'

'Yes.... What? No, don't do that. Perhaps I could see you tomorrow? You could – tell me again.'

He wrote down a number for her: 'If I'm not there, say who you are and they'll find me.'

He'd be working tomorrow. Of course. How strange. Everything going on. What had happened? 'Please go now.'

He went. She closed the door and turned back to the hall. This time it came up at her like a tide, humming, louder. It's true. It's over. It's finished. For ever. For ever. It reached her head and swirled round like acid turning her brain to broth. She fell on the stairs. It was not endurable. Her life was being taken from her and she was forced to watch, the stair-tread biting into her cheek, smelling the dust of the carpet: forced to move her head because the stair-tread hurt her cheek while she watched her life disappear. Then she had a visitation from Colm as he had been that morning, and she told him about this, the words growing out of her mouth like great flowers. She opened Sam's door and Cleo's, and stood looking in on them. But she had to close their doors again because of the noise that was coming out of her in great gasps that she couldn't control. She found herself in the bedroom – ties, shoes, a pair of trousers over the arm of a chair, a box of fifty cigarettes – a wave rose to its full height, balanced, toppled over her and she drowned. She fell on the bed, asleep as she fell. Around midnight Margaret rang, having heard, waking her. Somehow she convinced her she was all right. Now the pain really started, in the dark. Not worse, nothing could be worse, but now with time added, before it had been timeless, now time was waiting. What would she do with all the time that was left, impaled on those spikes? She stuffed a sheet into her mouth to stop herself crying out because she began to hear again the noise she was making.

10

I don't dwell on my own pain to make anyone sorry for me in particular but for all us human beings.

Toby told me again, afterwards, what had happened, told me about Colm's smile.

He did all the things that were necessary. I didn't go. They were nothing to do with Colm. Toby, this man Colm didn't know well, and I didn't know at all, came from nowhere, as often happens, and helped in the best way possible; he did all the practical things and said very little.

The other people I knew tried to help me forget. This astonished me. They were kind but stifling, I had to escape from them to be on my own. You should think about death when it happens near you. You'll have to think about it one day, so why not now? What about the dead? Are they not to be spoken of as if they've done something disgraceful? I understood why Colm had been so excited by the midnight mass in France when the fishermen had kissed each other and wept. We need ceremonies like that. Without them we are lost. We've thrown so many old things away, rightly I expect, but we have a hole where they were and we ought to be trying to fill it.

They gave a memorial concert of Colm's music. I was surprised how well known he was; but then of course he died young, which always makes people respectful. We are still very primitive, really.

Sometimes the man playing the piano took a long plank that covered all the keys and slammed it down in a great jangling chord. Other times he put ashtrays on the strings to give a tinny effect, or plucked at the strings themselves with what looked like a salt-cellar. Some people tittered, but the rest looked very serious. I felt sure Colm wanted them to laugh. I also felt, very strongly, that he wasn't there at the concert. Had no interest in it at all.

But the music was very like him. Sometimes a tune broke through the pops and clicks and bangs and the breathy poops from the wind-instruments, clear and happy and defiant; but there were seductive talkative snakes lying in wait, with horrible squirming yelps; the tune would rise above these, glassy and clear, until everything seemed about to be explained, it balanced, then some pull downwards made it topple into fragments again; the effort began to build up another wave, you felt it must succeed. Then the pianist banged the lid of the piano down, sharply, twice. That was the end, and it frightened me.

After that they played something, quite short, called 'Tent-flap', alert and beautiful like a praising competition between angels; there was no doubt in it, only joy. I suddenly saw how much Colm had believed. It wasn't the music he wrote but the music in life he tried to listen to, he didn't believe in silence but in a tune, a tune with words he strained to hear. He really believed in the Holy Ghost.

For the last piece they brought on a pin-table like the one in France and they must have rigged it in some way because at the right moment it joined in, went mad, pinging away, lights flashing as though every lit-up number had been hit at once and went on being hit. It wasn't just a trick, it worked, and everybody laughed. They'd left it till last because of the kind of thing it was. But it wasn't the last, the piece before had been that.

When it was over I saw Toby. He came up to me and said: 'He was very good, you know,' and I was pleased. Colm had told me he liked Toby because he didn't go in for 'flannel'. I left as quickly as I could because I didn't want to see anyone else who knew me and have to watch them struggle to think of something to say.

In the morning the papers were reverent. 'An original talent moving towards a greater profundity', 'A loss to British music' and so on. I cut them out to keep them, but then I threw them away. *Sad loss, full stop. On to the next.* That was not the way.

What was?

About this time people began to say: Look, you've had a dreadful time but you're young, etc. You've your life to live.

May I say something to anyone who has to deal with a

survivor? Please don't talk like that. Because it isn't *like* that. You're defining 'living' in the way that seems obvious to you; the experience of the survivor may have made him see things differently.

Of course there can be self-indulgence in grief, but the person you're trying to help will know where that begins sooner than you do. Perhaps *he* regards your distraction policy as self-indulgence. This business of 'living again'. Of course! Of course we must live, but the problem is to include the extra aliveness. This is bewildering. For months I saw colours (in grass a kind of blue) that I had never seen before. I was more alive than I had ever been because (and this is very hard to understand) of Colm's death. This awareness made the world I was invited back into look very drab. Maybe it is really shock, the new colours for instance, a clinical condition. Perhaps. But perhaps the shock is trying to tell us something and we should be allowed to listen because maybe it is news for us all. Sometimes when I was with people a river of laughter flowed right through me, clear and unstoppable, washing away everything unnecessary and distracting, like the laughter there is sometimes in the background of Mozart, behind those people singing in Così fan tutte. It was as far as possible from hysteria and I used to pray for it to come back, because at those moments I was nearer something that we all want to get nearer to whether we understand or not, nearer than I had ever been before, but it only comes when it wants to. When I tried to talk about any of this to friends, people who prided themselves on their unblinking facing up to 'things as they are' I saw them shy violently at this, different, kind of possibility. I didn't and don't blame them, but I'm sure they're wrong, now.

Anyway, I was disinclined to behave as though nothing has happened.

You can easily come to doubt the largeness of life but few can feel that way about death. Yet it is so pitiful – hospitals usually, 'arrangements', 'in ever fading memory of'. Why is what we feel so enormous, even if it is only fear? Even the guards in the camps, Colm told me, often took to drink, or had breakdowns. And although our knowledge of these camps has knocked our attitude to everything sideways that is *all the more reason for* insisting on what we also know is true. I believe there is no one who is not more startled than he can account for when he is in the presence of death. If this is true it throws a light back on life that we must use.

I was lucky to have Margaret to talk to; muddle, self-pity, new discoveries, horror, all jumbled up together; it didn't matter, she really listened because she wasn't scared. When I tipped over the edge and became maudlin and silly, she led me back.

She talked about herself too, which is one of the greatest gifts one person can give to another – trusting one sufficiently to reveal themselves.

One day she said to me, about Colm: 'I wonder if you really know how much he loved you?' I waited for her to go on: no one else would even mention Colm to me – as though it was indecent. 'I saw him looking at you once or twice and it made me happy just to see the expression on his face.' I'd seen that look. But you can begin to doubt things. There are devils in the dark as well as helpful angels. The joy of someone confirming it for you! There is no generosity like it. Why is it so rare?

I don't want to sound bitter. This is really a sermon, trying to help anyone who might read it not to make the same mistakes. I felt more in touch with people than I ever had before (they started talking to me about themselves and I listened, I'd learned from Margaret that is all that anybody ever wants, and if you listen they will tell you everything). But my friends behaved as though my situation was a disease I should be left alone with until it had worn off. As I say, there is something missing in our way of dealing with what is, after all, a very frequent and commonplace matter.

After a while I went to stay with my mother in New York – took the children for a holiday. She was on Number 4 at the time, a movie executive, but I never met him, he was always away and Ma spent most of the day on long-distance. She was just the same, still beautiful, still spending money as though the world was a toy-shop, her favourite toys were still men. She really loved them and I loved that about her. She could find an attractive man anywhere and find a man attractive for anything, his good looks or his wartiness, his virile strength or how sweet he looked in his bath-chair. We laughed so much together in that ghastly 100 dollars a day hotel apartment it was like being back with Simon. My mother filled the room with those hotel flowers that never look quite fresh, as though stolen from an expensive funeral. She always arranged a setting for herself like a Noel Coward play. It was when she was giving me worldly advice that I felt furthest from her, because that too had a period-flavour. She told me how she had suffered (I'm sure she had) and that love was what mattered, Love, Love, Love, women were born to suffer and Love – 'C'est moi qui parle'. I don't find this, as a philosophy for women, attractive or true. It wasn't that I felt superior, it was more as if we were never quite talking about the same thing, which is very tiring.

Then I heard that Charles Findus had been killed getting off a bus. I couldn't believe it but I've been told since that this sort of thing often happens. It's as though you tune into a wave-band that only broadcasts a certain kind of news. I went back to England to be with Margaret.

How well she took it.... By 'well' I don't mean only that she made no fuss. She'd earned the right to make none. She could afford to tread lightly on the surface because she hadn't been scared to look underneath, it wasn't the kind of deaf, death's head stoicism you can manage by putting cotton-wool in your ears, grinning and bearing it. She listened.

She talked about him so easily, and about what his absence meant to her; because pain had always been included in her way of seeing life she could laugh without her laughter having that terrible scoutmaster note. She cried sometimes. We cried together for our losses, they were the right kind of tears and that was due to her.

Margaret had loved Charles in a strange way, strange to me, with a kind of amused detachment.

'Charles knew his limits and moved inside them like a bird nesting. He was just like a bird, turning round and round making the nest fit him, then peering over the edge trying to look fierce and invisible at the same time. Heaven knows what he made of my dreaminess, he loved precision. But we were both after the same thing, I think.'

'What was that?'

She smiled: 'To find out who we were and live accordingly, I suppose. We tried to do it together.

'Charles saw you once on a bus, you know. He told me about it. A beautiful girl writing down her reasons for being faithful. He loved beautiful girls – used to peer at them particularly hard over the edge of the nest. And then, when we met on the beach....' We both began to laugh. 'Dear Charles ... I found some photographs.' She told me about the pictures of people making love she'd found in a drawer.

'Did you mind?'

She shook her head, still smiling. 'There are lots of things I didn't give Charles. There were things he didn't give me. Clearly I couldn't give him the whole of the female sex. That was his dream. An innocent one, really. We were on a journey together, he was entitled to his secrets, I had mine. We all want something more. Maybe that's what lust is ... a kind of prayer turned inwards.'

Simon came to see me once. It was my turn to feel embarrassed. He couldn't be expected to feel heartbroken, but his efforts to tread carefully were not his kind of thing, were painful to watch. He'd become involved with another model girl, an Australian as thin as Thin but more voluble, and after a while we dropped each other altogether. It was sad but not relevant at the time. We shall be easy with each other again one day.

People sometimes commiserated with me for not having a job to keep me occupied, as though 'work' was considered the normal escape from thought and feeling. But why should we want to escape these? In fact, I'd never worked so hard. There is a character in a book by Saul Bellow who counts suffering as work, and that's right. It also takes talent to suffer properly, more than I possess. But I don't want to emphasize the suffering: not because I want to be cosy. Like everyone else (I think) I'd wanted life to be important and now it was – because of death. It took me all my time and energy to try and work that out: how death, which is obviously the end, could seem so like a beginning. I'm not talking about a next life – I stop myself thinking about that until I know more, if I ever do. I'm unable to think of Colm as finished for ever, but if that proves anything one way or the other I do not know and try not to ask myself. When his death has cast such a bright beam on life it seems both silly and ungrateful to go peering about at the dark edges, ignoring what it has lit up in front of my eyes, sometimes so brightly that I am very far from understanding what I see.

But there remains suffering. There's no point in soldiering on, head down. We have to fight suffering by including it in our living, hating it for ourselves and for others. Margaret's mention of a journey was hard for me because I am younger than she is and it is hard to make one alone, or almost alone.

I saw a book in a shop window called *Look! We have come through!* That's it exactly! That's what I want to be able to say. I bought the book and I liked nearly all the poems but it is the title that has stuck in my mind.

The thing is that you have to say '*We* have come through!' to somebody who's done it with you. I'll never be able to do that, not to Colm, who's the person I started with.

As my friends say, I am young. I do 'have a life to live' and perhaps (which is what they mean) I'll meet a man and we'll be married and they can breathe easily again. But if it happens I shall never be able to say to him 'Look! We have come through!' There is always only one person we cry to, only one that the part of us which cries calls out to. This is the mystery, the one Colm's death throws a light on. A specialness connecting us with every other specialness, I mean with every other life, not because it is general and vague but because it is particular and irreplaceable. It isn't an answer to our lives, but it is the final sense of the importance of them, each in its own specialness. It's our beginning.

I know that wherever I am, here, still in this room filled with Simon's furniture, at the North Pole, at the edge of the world, alone or not, looking upwards, downwards, every whichway, there will be only one cry pulled out of the part of me that cries, and it's a cry which joins me to the whole world, a cry of perfect loss. Oh Colm –

More about Penguins

Penguinews, which appears every month, contains details of all the new books issued by Penguins as they are published. From time to time it is supplemented by *Penguins in Print*, which is a complete list of all books published by Penguins which are in print. (There are well over three thousand of these.)

A specimen copy of *Penguinews* will be sent to you free on request, and you can become a subscriber for the price of the postage. For a year's issues (including the complete lists) please send 30p if you live in the United Kingdom, or 60p if you live elsewhere. Just write to Dept EP, Penguin Books Ltd, Harmondsworth, Middlesex, enclosing a cheque or postal order, and your name will be added to the mailing list.

Some other books published by Penguins are described on the following pages.

Note: *Penguinews* and *Penguins in Print* are not available in the U.S.A. or Canada

Something in Disguise

Elizabeth Jane Howard

In this compulsive, entertaining novel, Elizabeth Jane Howard sets out to explore the personal and social interactions of a contemporary family with a charming candour. Alice – innocent, painfully shy and very lonely, who marries a man much older than herself to escape a home that is becoming a prison.

Oliver – handsome, intelligent, drifting through an endless series of careers and girls in a restless search for involvement.

Elizabeth – who discovers that love, for her, leads to unhappiness.

May, their mother, whose second marriage to Colonel Herbert Browne-Lacey turns out to be a terrible mistake, making her life a struggle to keep the peace between her children and her boring, self-important husband.

Herbert – her husband, who keeps secret liaisons with a woman in London, has a past that is suspect, and future plans for May that are highly dangerous.

Not for sale in the U.S.A.

Salvage

Jacky Gillott

Helena Pascall walks out on her headmaster husband and three children, and thumbs a lift from a man with an eye and ear for erring wives.

He thinks Helena just wants a one-night stand. But it isn't anything like as simple as that and during her runaway day, Helena sieves through a ferment of memories to explain herself to herself. Tight-lipped puritanical mother; precocious success as journalist in London; long affair with novelist. The agonies and ecstasies of having children; marriage to an over-understanding husband who fills the house with human strays.

'I want a liturgy, I want rules . . . and I've found none.'

Salvage is a virtuoso first novel. Jacky Gillott reaches out of Helena's situation to probe fundamental themes . . . love, betrayal, guilt, innocence, and to touch new places in the heart and imagination.

Not for sale in the U.S.A.

Nicholas Mosley

Impossible Object

A novel written not so much to tell a story – though it tells more than one and from more than one viewpoint – but to create a pattern as subtle, complex, and intriguing as the relationships which altogether make up life itself.

'Each of Nicholas Mosley's novels bears the marks of intense feeling – the sense of the value of love and the need to celebrate its value suffuses the work with such completeness. He has witnessed and recorded very lovingly the facts of love' – *The Times*

Accident

Stephen, forty, philosophy don. Charles, a novelist. Rosalind, Laura, Francisca – their English women. William, youth, aristocracy.
And Anna von Grutz und Leoben; Stephen's student, Charlie's adultery, William's fiancée . . . the *Accident* in their lives. 'We were all fascinated because of the nothingness about her.'

A car crash – William dies, Anna escapes. A novel, *Accident*, where past and present, terrors and hopes, are felt through the characters' eyes. Written by the 'I' of a needle, the novel *Accident*, through which the reader passes, verbally spellbound; a needle stabbed into the stuff of an Oxford summer. Nicholas Mosley, author, fighting to record reality, converts reader into witness. Witness of an *Accident*.

Also available
Assassins

Not for sale in the U.S.A.

Margaret Drabble

A Summer Bird-Cage

Two sisters. Bright, attractive Sarah, newly down from Oxford and now bed-sittering in London; and beautiful Louise, who has just made a brilliant marriage to the rich but unlikeable novelist Stephen Halifax. Despite a promising start things seem to be going badly.

The Millstone

Rosamund – independent, sophisticated, enviably clever – is terrified of true maturity. Then, ironically, her first sexual experience leaves her pregnant . . . Margaret Drabble shows how Rosamund faces up to a failed abortion and the trials of unmarried motherhood.

The Garrick Year

This novel takes the lid off a theatrical marriage; inside we find Emma, married to an egocentric actor playing a year's season at a provincial theatre festival, David, her husband – and Wyndham the producer. The mixture turns rapidly to acid.

Jerusalem the Golden

The girl from Northam was grateful to find herself accepted in London intellectual circles. She could become the golden girl and have real affairs with married men, just like in the novels.

The Waterfall

Jane Gray, poetess and failed wife, considered herself a disaster area. Until the husband of her alter ego, cousin Lucy, climbed into her bed.